MATEO & NICOLE

PALMERS OF COPPER CREEK BOOK ONE

NATALIE DEAN

DEDICATION

I'd like to dedicate this book to YOU! All of my wonderful readers that have been following my stories over the years.

Can you believe we are starting on the fourth Copper Creek family?! I hope you enjoy the Palmers of Copper Creek just as much as you've enjoyed the other close-knit families.

Thank you to my wonderful ARC Team who catches my errors for me and helps spread the word about my books.

And of course, I can't leave out my wonderful mother, son, sister, and Auntie. I love you all, and thank you for helping me make this happen.

Most of all, I thank God for blessing me on this endeavor.

ALSO BY NATALIE DEAN

CONTEMPORARY ROMANCE

Copper Creek Romances

BAKER BROTHERS OF COPPER CREEK

Copper Creek Romances Series 1

Cowboys & Protective Ways

Cowboys & Crushes

Cowboys & Christmas Kisses

Cowboys & Broken Hearts

Cowboys & Second Chances

Cowboys & Wedding Woes

Cowboys' Mom Finds Love

CALLAHANS OF COPPER CREEK

Copper Creek Romances Series 2

Making a Cowgirl

Marrying a Cowgirl

Christmas with a Cowgirl

Trusting a Cowgirl

Dating a Cowgirl

Catching a Cowgirl

Loving a Cowgirl

Marrying a Cowboy

KEAGANS OF COPPER CREEK

Copper Creek Romances Series 3

Some Cowboys are Off-Limits

Some Cowgirls Love Single Dads

Some Cowboys are Infuriating

Some Cowboys Don't Like City Girls

Some Cowboys Heal Broken Hearts

Some Cowgirls are Worth Protecting

Some Cowboys are Just Friends

Some Cowboys Fall for Hidden Stars

Some Cowboys Come Home for Christmas

Some Cowboys Brave the Flames

Some Cowboys Fight for Love

PALMERS OF COPPER CREEK

Copper Creek Romances Series 4

Mateo & Nicole

Sophia & Cameron (Coming soon!)

Roman & Olivia (Coming Summer of 2025)

∾

Miller Family Saga

BROTHERS OF MILLER RANCH

Miller Family Saga Series 1

Her Second Chance Cowboy

Saving Her Cowboy

Her Rival Cowboy

Her Fake-Fiance Cowboy Protector

Taming Her Cowboy Billionaire

BROTHERS OF MILLER RANCH SERIES BUNDLE

MILLER BROTHERS OF TEXAS

Miller Family Saga Series 2

The New Cowboy at Miller Ranch

Humbling Her Cowboy

In Debt to the Cowboy

The Cowboy Falls for the Veterinarian

Almost Fired by the Cowboy

Faking a Date with Her Cowboy Boss

MILLER BROTHERS OF TEXAS SERIES BUNDLE

BRIDES OF MILLER RANCH, N.M.

Miller Family Saga Series 3

Cowgirl Fallin' for the Single Dad

Cowgirl Fallin' for the Ranch Hand

Cowgirl Fallin' for the Neighbor

Cowgirl Fallin' for the Miller Brother

Cowgirl Fallin' for Her Best Friend's Brother

Cowboy Fallin' in Love Again

BRIDES OF MILLER RANCH, N.M. SERIES BUNDLE

Though I try to keep this list updated in each book, you may also visit my website nataliedeanbooks.com for the most up to date information on my book list.

CONTENTS

1

Nicole (Nikki) Reynolds

ikki wrung her hands as she stood before the larger-than-life house. She shouldn't be here. What had she been thinking, coming to Copper Creek? If anyone knew that she'd practically stalked Mateo to find out where he lived, they'd probably out her and send her packing.

The fact of the matter was that she'd moved to Colorado Springs five years ago, shortly after Paxton was born. She hadn't known what had happened to the hottest guy in high school after her *then* best friend had left him at the altar, but now she did.

Mateo Palmer had moved from Montana all the way down to Colorado—probably to escape the memories of his past. He'd done well for himself. Apparently, he'd managed to do well enough that all his siblings wanted to follow him. And they all lived *here*.

Was it so bad that Nikki followed Mateo on social media and discovered he'd be looking to hire a few people as his ranch expanded? She didn't think so. Cooking was a passion of hers, and if he was looking, it felt like fate.

A lump formed in her throat as she attempted to come up with what she might say to him. She needed a new job.

Desperately.

Her divorce had landed her with practically nothing. No place to stay, no job to provide for herself and her son. The worst part was that she'd come here on a whim. She'd driven all the way down from Colorado Springs on a wish and a prayer that Mateo wouldn't hold her past friendships against her.

Stomach roiling with her own sour memories, Nikki took a step toward the house. She'd come all this way. That was a lot of gas money. She had to at least try to convince him to hire her; otherwise, this trip was for nothing.

Her hand trembled as she lifted her fist to knock on the front door. She squeezed her eyes shut as she shifted her weight from one foot to the next, pleading with herself to stay still. What was the worst thing that could happen?

Mateo could glare at her and scream at her to leave his property, that's what. They might have been friends before, but now? She wasn't sure. It had been nearly a decade since they'd last seen each other. And she'd been friends with the woman who had cheated on him and left him at the altar on their wedding day.

She spun around to leave just as the door opened. One of Mateo's younger siblings stood there. She was young. Maybe early twenties? Her large, nearly violet eyes filled her pretty face, framed by black, luscious hair. She was breathtakingly beautiful, much like her brother. "Hello?" she asked.

"I'm sorry. This was a mistake," she mumbled. There were cars parked in and around the property. They might have guests. She hadn't been sure, but the moment this young woman opened the door, she could hear the laughter and chatter in the background.

Geez! She should have just sent Mateo a message through their social media.

"It's fine," the woman said with a smile. "Who did you need to see?"

Nikki shifted again, hating just how much she didn't belong. Where each and every Palmer looked like Latino or Latina royalty, here she was short with too many curves and dull brown eyes that matched her hair.

Growing up, she hadn't cared what others thought about her appearance. Caroline was the only one who mentioned it. But then, her friend had always been the long-legged, blonde beauty that was fit to grace the covers of magazines. To Caroline, a woman's worth was closely related to her appearance.

It was just one of many reasons why they hadn't spoken in over six years.

The woman still stared at Nikki, curiosity shining in her eyes. She tilted her head, studying Nikki as if she recognized her but couldn't place her. That was to be expected. The woman was several years younger than Mateo.

Before Nikki could make an excuse and dart away, the woman pulled the door open. "Everyone is out back. I'm sure you could find who you're looking for."

Everyone? There was definitely a party going on. But if there were several people here, maybe Nikki could ask Mateo her favor without an audience. People were bound to be distracted.

She chewed on her lips and glanced over to her car—her only means of escape. It was now or never. She had to do this for Paxton. It wasn't about herself anymore. It hadn't been for five years.

Nikki nodded. "Thank you."

The woman ushered Nikki into the house and through to the back, where the double doors were propped open. There were a few people visiting in the kitchen, plucking at chips and popping them in their mouths. Nikki recognized another member of Mateo's family simply by the way he looked as though he'd stepped down from the heavens. He flashed her a smile and a spark of recognition entered his features.

She'd always been bad with names, but this sibling was older. She wanted to say his name was Rowan or Roman. Something like that. He shifted his attention to the woman leading the way. "Izzie. You want me to get Mateo?"

Izzie glanced over her shoulder at him with confusion. "Why?"

Before he could say more, Nikki stepped closer. "I can go if he's not available. It looks like you're having a party—"

Izzie's focus snapped to her, and she waved a hand. "It's just a barbecue. It was too nice of a day not to enjoy it." She popped her hip out and seemed to study Nikki closer. "You need to see Matt? He's probably helping with the puppies."

Nikki nodded, her throat dry. She knew that's what they specialized in here. Mateo's social media focused more on the ranch than his personal life. She didn't even know if he had a girlfriend, but she knew that they were expecting a litter of puppies any day now.

Izzie's smile broadened. She glanced over at her brother once more. "I'll get him."

Her brother's focus didn't stray from Nikki even as she moved from the house and out onto the porch. There were more people than she'd expected. At least two dozen, if not more. If this was a small get-together, she didn't want to know what a big party was.

Hovering on the back porch, she took in the couples chatting as they milled around or were seated at the card tables set out on the lawn. The smell of burgers filled the air, along with the mild scent of spring. Her eyes scanned the yard until they landed on Mateo, and she froze.

He stood speaking to a couple who were seated on a picnic blanket a little ways away from the crowd of people nearby. He held a bundle in his hands as he spoke.

That smile of his could light up the world if the stars had gone out. He looked like he'd been carved out of marble and brought to life. Nikki looked away, hating how her crush was so easily rekindled. No one had compared to him when they were in high school. Back then, he'd been muscular as he worked alongside his parents at a ranch in Montana. He'd been a football star, too.

Every girl in school fawned after him, and most of the guys were jealous of the attention he got. But it wasn't just his looks that drew people in. The man had a certain charisma that couldn't be shaken. Even after Caroline had left him at the altar, he'd picked himself up and moved on.

"Nicole? Nicole Reynolds, is that you?"

She jumped, stifling a squawk that wanted to burst from her throat at his arrival. Before she had a chance to get her wits about her, he pulled her in for a hug. Nikki blinked, stammering as she attempted to pull back from him.

Mateo didn't seem to notice as he stepped away and laughed. "What are you doing in Copper Creek?"

Her heart leaped into her throat. There was no sign of animosity in his stare. He wasn't judging her for being friends with the woman who had broken his heart. Maybe her request would actually pan out. She offered him a shy smile and folded her arms. "I... er... I wanted to..." She shut her eyes tight and forced herself to show some degree of confidence. Straightening her shoulders, she stared up at him and lifted her chin, seeing as he was a full head taller than she was. "I need a job."

His brows lifted, his smile fading but only a little. "A job..." he drawled.

She nodded. "I noticed you were looking for a cook."

Just like that, his smile returned. He shoved his hands in his pockets as he leaned against the porch. He eyed her up and down, making her feel more vulnerable than if she'd been standing there stark naked. "I didn't know you knew how to cook."

Fighting the urge to run out of there screaming, she swallowed hard and nodded. "I went to culinary school. For about a year, I was working in a bakery in Colorado Springs. But four years ago, I left that job."

"And for the last four years?" he asked.

Why did everything he said seem to sound so sensual? She was losing her ability to think straight.

Nikki cleared her throat, choking back what she was going to admit. She wasn't sure if he'd give her the job knowing she had a kid. The position offered room and board. Not a fully furnished apartment. "My husband—*ex*-husband— didn't want me working." It was true. Dennis didn't like the idea of her working when she had a kid—even though the kid wasn't his. He'd said he was a provider and provide he did.

Thinking back on it, she wondered if it was just one more way for him to control her.

Shoving that thought aside, she forced a smile she prayed made her look more confident. "I'm ready to get back to work."

His eyes surveyed her, drilling, probing as if he might be able to read her thoughts. What was he thinking? Was he curious about Caroline? This little interaction must be like the worst kind of blast from the past. His lips quirked upward, and he raked a hand through his hair. "So, in the last ten years, you went to culinary school, got married, and now you're... here."

She motioned around them. "And in the last ten years, you've made a name for yourself as a renowned sheepdog breeder."

He cocked his head to the side and chuckled. "It's nice to see you again, Nicole."

"Nikki," she reminded. Nicole was what Caroline insisted on calling her. Nikki was what she was always called by her other friends in school and she thought it suited her better than Nicole.

"Nikki," he said, his voice smooth as silk.

Her heart thrummed at the sound of her name on his tongue.

"You're familiar with the requirements of the job?"

She nodded.

"And you think you can meet them."

"I know I can," she said steadier than anything she had said up to this point. "You won't regret hiring me. I guarantee it."

He chuckled. "Is that so?"

Once again, she nodded. "I'm a hard worker. I'll make

sure everything is in order every single day. I'll offer variety and quality, and I know how to budget when it comes to supplies—"

"Okay, okay." He laughed. "You've got the job."

Her eyes rounded. "Really?"

Mateo lifted a shoulder. "Sure. What are friends for?"

She beamed. "Right. What are friends for?"

His gaze locked with hers for a long, breath-stealing moment. All those fluttery feelings she'd had for him when they were teenagers came rushing back to the surface before she had a chance to stamp them out and suffocate them.

"It really is good to see you, Nikki," Mateo said with a huge smile. He moved closer to her and brushed his hand down her upper arm. For a split second, she expected him to pull her into another hug, but he didn't. He merely let his gaze linger before saying, "Come back on Monday. We'll give you the grand tour after we get you moved in." He brushed past her, and her skin felt like it was on fire from where his skin had touched hers.

The lump in her throat nearly choked her as she spun to watch him head down the steps and back to the people who were here for their impromptu barbeque.

She'd done it. She'd gotten a job!

Nikki stifled a squeal as she hurried back through the house. She didn't bother to speak to anyone on her way out, least they see how excited she was.

2

Mateo Palmer

Mateo turned just in time to see Nikki disappear into the house. He'd nearly invited her to stay for the barbecue. But something had held him back. It was probably the bittersweet nature of her arrival. With everything that had gone wrong in his life, she was a bright spot. She'd been the most real person he'd known in high school.

He'd liked to think that she was his friend, but if he were honest with himself, he had to admit their paths would never have crossed if she hadn't been friends with Caroline.

His ex's name was just as bitter in his mind as it was speaking it aloud. He'd promised himself he wouldn't talk about her nor give her any of his energy thinking about her. The woman was poison.

It had started long before he'd gotten engaged to her—long before she'd left him at the altar with a shattered heart.

He shook his head, forcing those thoughts from his mind and choosing to linger on the woman he'd thought about more than once over the last decade. Nicole Reynolds. There had been moments in his life when he'd wondered what it would have been like had he fallen for Nicole first. If he'd allowed himself to push aside the high school expectations of the football player falling for the head cheerleader, he might have seen what Nicole had to offer.

It was a cruel twist of fate that she was here.

Or maybe it wasn't cruel at all.

She was just as beautiful and vivacious as he remembered—with curves in all the right places. Her eyes were warm and inviting, like a hazelnut hot chocolate on the first snowy day of winter. The way her hair fell around her shoulders in soft waves had made him itch to run his fingers through them.

What would their lives have been like if he'd sought her out back then? Would they be married?

He sighed. This line of thinking never boded well for him. He always ended up feeling down about missing out on an opportunity for happiness.

If Caroline was the ice queen, then Nikki was a fairy princess who could only bring joy. They were opposites in every way, from their looks to their personalities. He'd definitely chosen wrong when he'd started dating Caroline.

A groan slipped from his lips as he stalked toward Daniel, Aria, and Sophia, dropping down on the blanket beside them. Sophia glanced up at him with a smirk that only a sister could master. "Was that Nicole Reynolds?"

Mateo grunted, setting his eyes on the puppy in Daniel's hands. "So what's it gonna be? You keeping it?"

Aria tugged the newborn from Daniel's arms. "We're

definitely keeping it. Thanks, cousin." She beamed up at him, nuzzling the tiny pup through the blanket.

Mateo glanced once more toward the house as if he expected to see Nicole standing there watching him. It was a ridiculous notion. She'd come here for a job, not to catch up. He hadn't even gotten a chance to ask her how she'd found her way to this part of the state. They'd both been raised in Montana. It was strange, and yet a thrill still raced through his chest at the thought that maybe this was what his heart had been waiting for.

"What did Nicole want?" Somehow, Sophia always knew what he was thinking. He didn't know how she did it, but she could see right past his defenses to the deepest parts of his soul.

He looked at his sister, noting the smug smirk on her lips. He knew that look. She was planning something. Mateo rolled his eyes. Fat chance she'd be successful in whatever it was. "She needs a job."

Sophia lifted her brows, surprise lacing her features. "Really? Did you give her one?"

He arched an eyebrow. "What do you think? We haven't had any interest in the cook position. And that's what she's wanting."

At least Sophia looked pleased. She glanced at Daniel and their cousin with a knowing look—one that said they knew her plans. He had half a mind to ask them what it was all about, but a small part of him thought he already knew. Sophia had been trying for years to set him up with someone who could mend the broken pieces of his heart that Caroline had left behind. She'd failed time and time again. Well, maybe this prospect would be the one to get past his defenses.

A small smile tugged at Mateo's lips. It wouldn't be the worst thing to find love again—especially with someone like Nikki. He was due something good. Between his failed engagement and the issues his cousin had been through with her abusive father and controlling ex, they needed something to help them feel like their lives were getting better.

If that meant Sophia wanted to play matchmaker? So be it.

He leaned back on his hands and glanced between some of his favorite people. "We're having a dinner tomorrow with just the family. I want to go over the plans for the expansion now that the wrangler's cabin is complete and they're putting the finishing touches on the kitchen. For the most part, everyone will still be doing their usual work with the dogs." He turned to Daniel. "Since you'll be spearheading the wranglers, I'll need to speak to you more about picking someone to help with the cattle side of things. I know we're not going to be the top cattle-producing ranch in this part of the state, but I want to make sure what we do offer is top of the line, just like what we offer with our dogs."

"Just so long as the dog part of the business remains the focus, I don't care." Sophia shrugged. "We all agreed that we would specialize in that when we moved out here with you. Otherwise, we might as well have stayed behind with Mom and Dad."

"Mom and Dad don't own the property that they work in Montana," Mateo said, not needing to remind her. "You didn't come out here for the dogs, and you know it. This was our own slice of prosperity—our own future we were building."

Sophia's flat expression held a hint of amusement. "Yeah, okay. And there was that part, too."

"It's gonna be really different with a bunch of other guys underfoot. Not even Daniel's ranch has a lot of other men working the property. We're going to need to show that we're capable so they all stay in line."

Everyone gave a nod of agreement. Aria had chosen not to return to her hometown in Georgia because of her love of the country out here. She'd offered to focus on creating a webpage for Winding Creek Ranch as she continued with her freelance writing. There was talk of her looking into veterinary school as well.

Mateo glanced toward Daniel and offered him a smile. "I want you to know that if you choose to move on to a career in architecture after you're done with your schooling, I won't stand in your way. But there will always be a job here for you if you'd like."

Daniel held out his hand, and they shook as he grinned right back. "Why not do both?"

Mateo laughed. "Well, in that case, I might have to make a few requests after graduation. My family has already said they intend on sticking around, and there's no way we can raise six families in that house over there." He jerked his chin toward the house he shared with his brothers and sisters. "It's already feeling cramped as it is."

Sophia nodded. "I call dibs on the first house. I want one built over at the crest of the hill on the northern side of the property."

Mateo got to his feet as Sophia continued describing her dream home to Daniel, even though Mateo had a feeling the guy just wanted some time with his girl. He hadn't missed the ring on Aria's finger. There would be a wedding in the near future, and Mateo couldn't wait for it. The more good news they got, the better.

THEIR FAMILY DINNER WENT WELL. Each of his brothers and sisters approved of the changes he wanted to make in order to see their business prosper. It was a lot to be the leader of this family—to show strength even after everything they'd gone through. But he'd risen to the challenge and would continue to do so. No one could bring him down. He'd already hit rock bottom in his life, and he had no intention of going back.

An arm tugged him from the hallway into the downstairs office. Sophia faced him in the darkened room and lowered her voice. "Okay, spill."

He pried her hands from his upper arms and smirked. "Spill what?"

"Tell me what happened with Nikki? I know you're hiding something."

He snickered. "I'm not hiding anything. She came for a job. That's it."

"Come on. I saw the way you two were together. What did you say? What did she say?"

Mateo gave her a gentle push. "She said she needed a job. She's just gotten out of a bad marriage and wanted a change or something." Wait, did she say a *bad* marriage? Or had she just said she was divorced? Maybe he'd inferred the *bad* part.

Sophia gave him a shove in the chest and he yelped, not realizing he'd allowed himself to get lost in thought again.

He rubbed at the spot with a wince as he glowered at his sister. "What was that for?"

"She's divorced?" Her smile was even wider than it was yesterday when she'd asked about Nikki the first time. "So, she's single."

Mateo sighed. "Look, sis. I get that you want to help or whatever, but I don't need you to play matchmaker." His words were so contrary to his thoughts from before that he nearly grimaced. They weren't honest. He just didn't want Sophia to think that he was completely on board with whatever she had planned.

"Who said I'm playing matchmaker?" Sophia drawled, still smiling at him. "Maybe I'm just curious why your ex's best friend showed up out of nowhere. Did she mention 'she who shall not be named'?"

Mateo groaned, shoving past her. "No. And I didn't ask. There's no reason to bring her up or even think about her at this point. It's been ten years. I'm more than happy to leave that memory good and buried. I refuse to give her any more power than she's already gotten."

He headed down the hallway and paused before turning to face his sister, who had followed him a few steps.

"If you're so curious about Nikki, ask her yourself. She'll be moving in on Monday next week. I'm sure she would love the company."

"Maybe I will," Sophia called after him.

Mateo lifted a hand in the air, dismissing her from their conversation.

3

Nikki

Once again, Nikki was second-guessing the decisions she'd made. She hadn't told anyone that she would be bringing her son with her, and she was beginning to realize just how bad that was.

What if Mateo rescinded his job offer? It wasn't like she could keep the job and find a place to live in town. She'd barely had enough money to put gas in her tank for the drive over. How on earth was she supposed to have enough money for the first month, last month, and deposit?

That's why she needed this job so badly.

She glanced in the rearview mirror at her adorable little boy, who would have scowled at her had she called him that to his face. Paxton was five years old going on fifteen. He'd endured more in his life than some kids, though overall, she liked to think that he'd had it pretty good so far.

At worst, he'd lost the man who he'd grown up believing

was his father. Dennis had never officially adopted Paxton. He said it would feel weird in case Paxton's father did end up showing up out of nowhere.

It didn't matter that there wasn't a father's name on Paxton's birth certificate. It didn't matter that the man who'd sired her son hadn't been heard from since the day she'd announced her pregnancy.

Dennis didn't want to take on that responsibility.

In hindsight, she should have known something was wrong—or, at the very least, that her marriage wouldn't last —for that fact alone.

Paxton had been two when she'd gotten married. Dennis was the only father he knew, and it broke her heart that he had to experience this kind of abandonment.

As if he felt her gaze on him, he lifted his eyes to meet hers. She'd told him that they'd get him an air mattress with her first paycheck, and he'd be staying in the same room as she was. Hopefully, it would be large enough. Maybe she could even ask Mateo for an advance and get a bunk bed.

Her sweet, sweet boy smiled at her with encouragement. He hadn't wanted to leave his friends in Colorado Springs, but he'd been more than excited to meet some new people and be closer to horses.

Paxton sat straighter in his seat and peered out the window, his eyes rounding into saucers. "Is this the ranch we're going to live at?"

She nodded, twisting in her seat to face him. "This is the place. We'll have a few months before you start kinder-garten, so you get to explore first."

His smile eased some of the ache in her chest. Thank goodness children were resilient. Or maybe it was just

Paxton. It was moments like this when she felt she could take on the world as long as he was smiling just like that.

Nikki let out an uneasy breath, which drew Paxton's attention. "I need to tell you something, buddy."

His brows creased, and a small frown marred that beautiful face. "What's wrong?"

"The people here don't know you are coming." She hated the way his frown deepened, and she pushed past her worries that he felt unwanted or that he'd get in trouble. "But you know what?" she murmured. "They're going to love you."

That brought the smile right back. She wanted to add to what she'd said—telling him not to worry if people made any comments—but she didn't want to add more worry to an already unsettling day.

She got out of the car and walked around to the back door where Paxton was seated, then helped him out. They didn't have much in the way of clothes and belongings as they were still trying to figure out where to put everything. Dennis had agreed to let them gather their stuff over the next couple of months, but Nikki wasn't sure how patient he'd be if it took too long.

When she shut the car door and turned around, her worries were confirmed. Several people, who had previously been milling around back and forth from their own vehicles to the building where most of the men would be staying, had stopped. Their eyes were trained on Nikki at first but had immediately dipped to Paxton.

She reached for his hand and held onto it firmly before she tugged him around to the trunk for their suitcases. The only person who could kick her out was Mateo. And right now, he was nowhere to be seen. She didn't care what everyone else was thinking. All she needed to do was take Paxton into their living quarters and get situated so there was less of a chance they were turned away. She just had to prove that there was enough room for them to share a space.

Mateo had sent her a message letting her know that he'd arranged for her to have her own room at the wranglers' cabin, and she'd thanked him graciously. No one could complain about her son if she wasn't encroaching on their space, right?

With her hand still firmly holding Paxton's and the other gripping her suitcase handle, she turned toward the building. She kept her head held high as she moved past everyone gawking at her and toward the front door.

Unfortunately, a tall beast of a man stepped into her path. Arms folded, he stared down at her with an unwavering scowl. She'd thought Mateo was tall. But this man? He had to be at least a couple inches taller than Mateo. And he was built like a tractor.

She brought herself up short and sucked in a sharp breath.

The man's eyes slid to Paxton. "No children are allowed on the premises."

Nikki snorted. "I haven't heard of that rule."

Incredulity flickered in his eyes. "You'd want to subject your child to a building full of men who don't have any reason to hold their tongues or behaviors?"

She released her suitcase handle and placed a hand on her hip. "If you think Mateo would put up with the sordid behavior you're referencing, you're working for the wrong man."

The cowboy's head pulled back in surprise. She thought for a second that a smile tugged at his lips, but when she looked closer, she found that she was mistaken. He shook his head. "Even if that was the only issue, the room you've been assigned is too small. Children need space."

Tugging Paxton to the front of her and placing her hands on his shoulders, she stood her ground. "Better to be in a cramped room than on the street."

Finally, she saw some hesitation in his stance. Whoever this man was, he'd been hired to oversee the wranglers. Well, she wasn't a wrangler. She was the cook, and until Mateo told her to get lost, she'd be sticking around. She lowered her voice, uncaring that Paxton was witness to all of this. "Please. Just let us by so we can settle in."

"Mateo isn't going to like it," he mumbled, his expression softening as he took Paxton in one more time.

"You don't have to tell him right away. I'm sure he's too busy to have to deal with any of this. And Paxton knows how to keep himself busy." Geez! Now she was pleading with the guy—the very same one she'd not moments ago told herself wasn't in charge.

He scrubbed at his jaw and glanced toward the main house. It was too far away for them to see details of anyone coming or going. If Mateo was out on the porch, he'd have to strain his focus in order to notice something was amiss.

Finally, the cowboy gave her a curt nod. "I won't tell him, but you're going to have to deal with him when he finds out. The rest of the wranglers won't be showing up until tomorrow, so make sure your boy doesn't get underfoot when they arrive."

She glanced around at those who had been coming and going from the building, and in answer to her curious stare, the cowboy said, "These guys are just getting furniture and other necessities moved in."

Nikki nodded, relief pooling in her stomach. As long as Paxton stayed out of sight for the next couple of days, she knew she'd be able to keep him here. She couldn't see Mateo sending them away after they'd settled in. He wasn't heartless.

Smiling at the cowboy, she held out her hand. "Thank you…"

He took her hand in his, engulfing it almost entirely. "Daniel." He jutted his chin in a direction off to the side. "My fiancée lives in a cabin on that side of the property. I'm there often for dinner, so I'll be just a door down from you."

"And when you're not?"

His first genuine smile transformed his face into something that could make a woman's heart melt, and that familiar stirring of longing filled her chest. Not for Daniel—but to have someone in her life that could make her feel whole again. "I grew up about ten minutes from here. I live on a ranch with my brothers and sister." He thumbed over his shoulder. "I'll show you to your room." His focus skittered over Paxton again and that concern returned to his gaze, but he didn't say anything more.

Daniel had been right. The room was barely big enough to put a twin air mattress on the floor next to the existing bed. They'd be cramped but safe and warm. She would take this over homelessness any day.

There wasn't much to unpack. Paxton pulled a few toys from a backpack she'd brought in for him, and he played on the bed.

"I'm going to check around this place and see if I can find a notebook to plan the menu, okay, kiddo?"

He nodded, not looking up.

"You need to stay here. I don't want you wandering around."

At that, he did meet her eyes. "Because I'm not supposed to be here." It wasn't really a question.

Her heart lurched and guilt plagued her. He'd have more freedom after they settled in. "It's just for now," she assured him. "Just until we get our feet on firm ground."

Paxton nodded, turning back to his toys. Nikki moved out of the room, shutting the door behind her.

She found her way into the kitchen and smiled. It wasn't large, but it didn't have to be. From what she understood, there was a larger space for meals. This was just where the wranglers could snack or get a quick bite. She couldn't wait to get a tour of the space where she'd be working.

Nikki pulled open a couple cabinets and drawers, but did not find a notebook where she could begin her planning. She'd have to request that Mateo get her one.

"There's the star of the show."

She jumped, bumping her head against a cupboard door as she turned at the familiar voice.

Mateo leaned against the doorway like it was the most natural thing in the world. He grinned at her, his eyes sparkling with mischief. Why was he looking at her like that? And why did it make the skittery feelings in her stomach get worse?

Nikki swallowed thickly, beating down the blush that threatened to flood her face and offered a nonchalant smile at him. "I'm hardly the star."

He pushed away from the wall, prowling toward her. "I beg to differ. Aria's a great cook, but she prefers making food just for her and Daniel. It's sorta their thing. My sisters can cook, but you can only eat so many bits of eggshells before you start second-guessing your life's choices."

Laughter spilled from her lips, and his smile brightened.

Mateo leaned against the counter, his eyes never leaving her face. "Do you know how long it's been since I've had a really good home-cooked meal?"

"How long?" she said.

"Too long." The way he was looking at her—the way he was speaking to her—it was messing with her head in a way that was not appropriate at all.

Okay, this was just how Mateo was. He wasn't being inappropriate with her, but the reaction she was feeling definitely was.

He was her boss! She couldn't allow herself to become a weak, simpering fool who fell for a man simply because he was gorgeous and charming as all get-out. She wouldn't jeopardize her job by making things complicated.

4

———

Mateo

Mateo drank her in. Nikki wore a lightweight sweater and a pair of jeans that hugged every curve of her body. Her hair was pulled back into a haphazard bun atop her head. He knew enough about that style to know it took a lot of work to make it look effortless.

She didn't wear much makeup. Rather, she leaned into her natural beauty—something that he had a tendency to be drawn to, especially after dating Caroline.

And that laugh!

He could listen to that laugh every day for the rest of his life.

Based on the way she'd pulled back from him so both the kitchen island and the space around it stayed between them, he could tell she was keeping her distance. There were a multitude of reasons that would make sense. The fact that they weren't exactly close and her friendship with his ex were just a couple of them.

Mateo cocked his head, eyeing her from where he stood. It was funny, really. He'd thought seeing someone from his past would send him into a downward spiral, but that didn't happen. Either so much time had passed that he'd scarred over and couldn't feel the pain anymore, or it was Nikki.

She flushed and a smile spread across her face. "What?"

Right. He'd been staring. He probably shouldn't be doing that. "How do you like your room? I know it's not much, but—"

"It's perfect," she blurted. "It's exactly what I needed." Her blush deepened as she moved closer to him. "But I did need to ask you for something."

"Anything," he uttered the word before he realized how it might sound.

Nikki paused only briefly before she nodded. "Great. I want to get a menu planned. I'm sure you have some basic ingredients in the kitchen ready for meals, and I'd like to take stock. Then I can place some orders for specific meals I'd like to put on the menu. I'll need a notebook—"

"Notebook? Old-school, huh?" He chuckled.

She didn't respond with the same lighthearted sound. Instead, her brows pulled together. "Do you... recommend something else?"

He shrugged. "I figured you'd use a computer or something."

"Oh..." Her voice trailed off, and she pursed her lips together for a moment. "I don't have a computer. Do you have a system in place already?"

Mateo shook his head. "But if you'd like one, I'm sure we could get something worked out. Do you need a computer?"

She blinked at him like his suggestion was absurd. "I would never ask you to—"

"It's part of the job, right? I can't exactly ask you to cook a meal without an oven."

"But a computer is different," she said. "I could just use a regular old notebook—"

"I'll get you one from the house. But I'll also order you a laptop that you can use to keep track of what we have. It'll be easier to keep things digital."

The way her face lit up with excitement did something to him that he hadn't experienced in a long time. Maybe it was the fact that they had a familiarity with one another. Or perhaps it was the fact that he'd harbored a secret attraction to her all those years ago. Either way, he wasn't going to question it too much.

Everything would stay professional. It didn't matter that she stirred emotions in him that he'd long since thought were dormant. She was his employee, and he knew better than to allow himself to get wrapped up in something that wasn't appropriate.

"So, Nikki, you want to catch me up on… stuff?"

She snickered. "What kind of stuff?"

Mateo shrugged. "You know. Stuff. You still see a lot of people from high school?"

"If you mean Caro—"

He snapped up straighter. "No. I mean people from the football team. Classes." It was painstakingly obvious that he didn't want her to even mention the woman who had broken his heart. And that was proof enough that he wasn't completely over the heartache.

Did he miss Caroline? No way. If he never saw her again, it would be too soon. In fact, he'd blocked her from every social media account he had, as well as his phone. Caroline West was dead to him.

Nikki definitely noticed his change in posture, and she took a startled step back when he'd straightened. She pulled her lower lip into her mouth and chewed on it as her eyes sought out anything else in the room other than him. She cleared her throat and shook her head. "Not really. I moved away from Montana about six years ago. I told you I got a job at that bakery..." Her eyes darted away from him, never staying on him long enough for him to get a read on her.

"Yes, you mentioned that. Then you were married to a guy who didn't want you working. Anything else happen? Any life-shattering experiences?" He grinned at her, letting his voice charm her. He was good at this side of things. Most women loved to open up to him because he was a good listener.

She shifted and her focus darted to the doorway. He glanced over his shoulder and frowned. Was she wanting to escape him already? He hadn't thought he was making her uncomfortable.

Slowly, he dragged his gaze back to meet hers. "So, no life-altering changes that you want to share?" He leaned against the countertop again and smiled. "Okay, I'll go then." He tapped his finger on his chin. "After I made the biggest mistake of my life in loving the wrong woman, I got left at the altar. So I moved out here—with my brothers and sisters. We wanted to start a business that was all our own."

Nikki seemed to be drawn into his story—which was strange because if she was connected with him through social media, she would already know all of this. It was part of their story.

"All of us have always loved dogs. We got a good taste of

them back home, where my parents work on a ranch for a really good family, the Millers. We figured we'd make a life out of it. So, we pooled our resources together and bought this piece of land."

"But some of your siblings are so young."

He nodded, grinning wider. "When they turned sixteen, they begged my folks to let them come down here to finish their schooling and run this place with me. Sophia and I started the whole thing, and the rest of them followed."

"And you never..." Her voice trailed off again.

Mateo waited for her to finish her thought, but when she wouldn't, he didn't push the issue. "It's worked out pretty well so far. We've made a name for ourselves in Copper Creek and some of the surrounding areas. People don't just buy the dogs we breed for herding their animals. They use them for protection. We run things very humanely. Our dogs aren't allowed to have more than two to three litters. Their health is the most important thing to us. Last year, Sophia and I decided that we wanted to do something more with our land, so now we're expanding. We have some cattle, and we're going to be training more horses along with the dogs. We have a lot in the works, and ultimately, I'd like to be the top provider for cattle dogs and horses that work with them. The folks around here have said a handful of times how they like the idea of their horses being trained alongside their dogs."

"That's an interesting idea for sure," she said, eyes still alight with fascination. "I can't wait to see what you make of it."

They shifted from that conversation to a couple other topics before Nikki asked, "How many men have you hired? And will I be cooking for more than them?"

"More than them?" he asked.

She nodded. "You mentioned you'd be interested in trying my cuisine."

His smile returned. "Oh, right. I'm not sure, actually. I haven't asked my family if they're going to take advantage of us having our own cook on the property. But I would expect they'll be stopping by. We've never had someone to cook for us in a professional capacity."

"Well, I hope that I meet your expectations." She laughed. "It's been a while since I cooked for more than a couple people. My skills might be a little rusty."

Mateo wasn't sure when it happened. All he knew was one moment they were on opposite sides of the island, and now they were leaning against it, side by side, as they chatted like they'd always been friends. The side of his arm brushed up against the side of hers as they spoke.

Nikki started into a story about what it was like learning at a real culinary school and how different it had been to find work at a bakery. "The one thing that remained a constant was having to rise early. In order to have fresh bread, you have to start on it hours before the sun comes up."

"Makes sense. But I'm not going to ask you for fresh bread daily. That just sounds cruel."

She laughed. "It's no bother. It's actually one of my favorite things to do when I can't sleep."

"And why wouldn't you be able to sleep?" he asked, genuinely concerned. If she was dealing with her own sort of heartache like he had, he wouldn't hesitate to track down this ex of hers and show him just what kind of man disposes of a woman as wonderful as he remembered Nikki being.

Nikki didn't look up at him as her features scrunched

with something that almost looked like guilt. He turned to face her, itching to lift her chin to have her tell him everything. He wanted to take away that ache deep inside her and replace it with thoughts of confidence and joy.

Mateo refrained from touching her, but he didn't ease up on his question. "Nikki," he said. "Is everything okay?"

Before she could lift her eyes to meet his, the sound of light, quick footsteps shuffled down the hallway and headed right for them. Strange. They didn't sound like any animal he'd ever heard. Nor did it sound like an adult man—so it wasn't going to be Daniel.

Nikki's eyes widened larger than he'd ever seen just moments before a kid burst into the kitchen.

"Mom. Guess what?"

A little kid!

Mateo only vaguely noticed the way Nikki tensed beside him as he stared at the young boy in question. Where had he come from? What was he doing here?

Wait a minute.

Mom?

With slow movements, Mateo turned his head to face Nikki, finding her as pale as the fresh eggshell-colored paint on the walls in the kitchen.

Mom.

This kid belonged to her. Nikki was a mother. And she hadn't told him.

He swiveled his attention from Nikki to the boy and back again. "Did you forget to tell me somethin'?"

The boy seemed to have suddenly realized he'd done something he wasn't supposed to. Of course, he did. The way his mother looked, like she might pass out at any given moment.

Mateo frowned. "Nikki," he whispered in warning. One thing he wouldn't put up with was lying. Caroline had lied. She'd cheated, and she'd left. Mateo refused to spend time with people who couldn't be honest with him, and yet here he was, standing next to a woman who hadn't told him she had a kid.

"He can't stay here."

5

─────────

Nikki

Tears stung in Nikki's eyes as she gaped at Mateo. She couldn't hold back her emotions as she blustered at him. "What? Why?"

Mateo folded his arms tightly against his chest, fury flickering in his gaze as he turned a sharp stare on her. She wanted to shrink away from it, but she couldn't move. He had her pinned with his eyes in a way that didn't quite make sense.

She attempted to ask again, motioning to Paxton to hurry to her side as if she could shield him from what was happening. "Show me where it's against the rules to have my son here. You can't just fire me because I have a child. That's against the law."

For a moment she thought he might sneer at her—tell her that she wasn't technically hired until he filed the paperwork and got her tax information in order. But he didn't.

The slew of emotions that ripped through her was achingly painful. She'd gone from disgruntled to being in denial, and already she was ready to drop to her knees and plead for him to let them stay. She needed this job. She needed to get out on her own and take care of her son, and no one wanted to hire a woman who had been absent from the workforce for as long as she had. "Please, Mateo," she whispered, her fingers digging into Paxton's shoulders until a surprised sound escaped him. "I need this job. *We* need it."

They both looked down at her son, and Mateo shook his head. "I didn't mean I was going to fire you. But he can't stay here." He gestured to the wrangler's cabin. "As much as I'd like to say it wouldn't bother me, I can't in good conscience allow a child to live under the same roof with several men who don't have completed background checks. If something happened to him, I'd be liable."

"But I can't afford to live anywhere else—at least not until I get a few paychecks—"

He cut her off simply by turning his back on her and heading toward the door where Paxton had materialized. She scrambled after him, taking Paxton's hand in her own.

"I'm sorry, Mom. I forgot."

She gave a loving, patient look to her son. "It's not your fault, sweetheart," she whispered, "I shouldn't have taken so long." She'd gotten so wrapped up in her conversation that she'd let herself forget that she'd only come out of her room in search of a notebook.

Mateo stopped in front of her door and pushed it open. His gaze swept through the small area, and his frown deepened considerably before he motioned to it with disgust. "Aside from the other men who will be staying in this building, I can't see how you'd think you could live in here comfortably. This space is only meant for one person."

She pulled Paxton against her front and scowled at Mateo, repeating what she'd told Daniel. "It's better than living on the street or in a shelter."

Mateo's frown intensified. He shook his head and pulled out his phone.

She watched with horror as he lifted it to his ear. Who was he calling? Was Daniel going to get in trouble? Would he go so low as to contact child protective services? "Who are you calling?" she demanded.

"I need to talk to you," he said into the phone.

Paxton lifted his face so his eyes met Nikki's, and she brushed at a tear before he was able to see it.

"Yeah," Mateo barked, still talking on the phone. "I changed my mind. If that's what you want, you can have it. For the life of me, I don't get it, but something's changed."

He was giving her position away. That was the only thing that made sense.

Mateo hung up his phone and pointed to their room. "Pack your things."

"Mateo—" she stammered. "Don't do this—"

He stopped suddenly, understanding suddenly filling his vision. "I'm not firing you," he practically growled. "But you really should have told me about..." His eyes dipped to Paxton, and he heaved a sigh before he dropped to a crouch and flashed her son the biggest smile he had. "Do you like horses?"

Paxton's concern immediately fled from him, and he nodded with a grin. "They're my favorite animal. They're so fast."

"What do you say I take you out to meet a cowboy while your mother and I have a chat?"

Paxton frowned once more and looked from Mateo to his mother.

She nodded. What else could she do? She didn't want Mateo to fire her in front of her son. Paxton would only blame himself.

Mateo rose, ruffling Paxton's hair before he gave Nikki a firm look.

The second they were packed, Mateo handled the luggage and guided them out to the barn, where Daniel met them. He nodded to Paxton. "I want you to show the kid around. Let him meet the best horses."

Daniel's eyes dipped down to Paxton, and he grinned. Just before he disappeared into the barn, he tossed Nikki a worried look.

The world was falling out from under her. The ground shifted and rocked, threatening to make her stumble as Mateo led the way toward the main house. His office was located there. He was going to have privacy to reprimand her for lying about her son.

She should have just told him when she'd come asking for the job. Maybe she could plead her case better if her son wasn't there watching everything fall apart.

Unfortunately, she didn't feel she had a good shot at being successful.

Mateo continued walking, the suitcase in his hand, as they climbed a set of stairs and headed toward the end of a hallway. A door was ajar, and he pushed it open, revealing not an office space but a spacious bedroom with two twin beds.

"I..." Her throat closed up. "I don't understand."

Mateo put the suitcase just inside the room and leaned his back against the doorjamb, blocking her from escaping. His expression was cool, unreadable. Gone was the flirty, happy guy she'd been chatting with.

She got the distinct feeling that she'd hurt him by not telling him everything.

"You'll stay here."

She gasped, whirling around to face him after getting another good look at the bedroom. "I can't."

"You can, and you will. Honestly, I didn't like the idea of you staying in a building full of men. I'd anticipated hiring a male cook, but..." He lifted a shoulder, and a hint of a smile tugged at his lips. "You made an offer that I couldn't refuse."

Heat flooded her body as she once again took in the bedroom. "I can't," she repeated. "This room—it must belong to one of your brothers. Or two of them."

Mateo nodded, not leaving from where he relaxed in the doorway. "This is Marcus's room. He's my youngest brother. Sometimes, he shares the room with cousins who come to visit. Sometimes, he shares it with Roman when we have a guest who needs their own room."

Nikki shook her head again. "But—I really don't want to impose. Where will Marcus stay? He needs a space—"

"He wanted to move into the wrangler's cabin." Mateo smirked. "Heaven knows why. I'm guessing he's tired of sharing a house with our sisters. They can be... a bit much."

"But you didn't want him to." That much was clear. Otherwise, Marcus would have already been moved out to the cabin.

Mateo pushed off the door and moved closer to her, making the room feel ten times smaller. "I wanted him to be with his family because there's nothing more important."

His eyes burned into her with an intensity that made her shiver. "You should have told me you have a son, Nikki. I wouldn't have turned you away. There's nothing more beautiful than a mother who would be willing to do anything for her child."

Those shivers turned into tumultuous waves of chills as they coursed beneath her skin. His voice was so quiet, so sure that she could do nothing but agree with him. "I'm sorry," she whispered. "You're right. I should have told you."

He nodded, his smile returning to its usual place. "Good. Now that we have that covered, I want to talk to him. Based on the way you were behaving, I wouldn't be surprised if he thinks I'm the big bad wolf at this point." He motioned toward the door. "Ladies first."

Her lashes fluttered as her heart tripped over itself. This was the Mateo she'd gotten to know back when they were in high school. This was the man who could make any number of girls fall all over themselves just to catch his eye. He treated everyone like they were the most important person in the world, so the fact that he was talking to her like this didn't mean anything.

Not a single thing.

She nodded, reveling in the way her taut, aching muscles had finally relaxed.

Mateo hadn't fired her. He totally could have—or rather not gone through with the hiring process. She didn't have the money to fight him on it in court, and she would have been left to find another option, even though she'd been searching for weeks before she'd finally come here.

Nikki focused on her breathing as they left the house and headed to the barn. Daniel and Paxton exited the structure a moment before they reached it, and he came barreling toward her.

His arms wrapped tightly around her legs, and he peered up at her with concern. "Is everything okay?"

She feathered her fingers through his hair and nodded. "Everything is fine. Mr. Palmer here has just found us a different place to stay."

Paxton pulled back and gazed up at the other tall man in their presence. His head craned upward, and he looked as though he expected Mateo to take a big bite out of him if he got too close.

Mateo chuckled and dropped down to be at eye level with the boy. He held out his hand. "Did you know that I'm trying to build a bigger ranch out here? That's why I needed your mother. There are going to be lots of mouths to feed, and from what I hear, she's the best cook."

Paxton didn't miss a beat. He nodded firmly and folded his arms. "She's the best cook ever. She makes the yummiest mashed potatoes."

Mateo cut a look in Nikki's direction. "Is that so?"

She flushed and let out a soft laugh as she waited for Paxton's response.

"Yeah."

Mateo chuckled. "Well, then I'm guessing we're going to have to have a lot of potatoes on the menu. What do you think?"

Paxton nodded resolutely.

"You know what else?" Mateo said, turning serious. "I'm going to need lots of help around here this summer. A *lot* of help. I might even need to hire a few more cowboys." He seemed to let those words sink in, and then he leaned forward almost conspiratorially. "Do you think you could help me out with that? Can you be a cowboy?"

Paxton frowned and dropped his hands to his sides. "I don't have a hat. Or boots."

Mateo tossed back his head with a laugh. "I'm sure I could fix that. Here." He pulled his hat from his head and placed it on Paxton's head. It was too large, but Paxton practically glowed from beneath it.

Nikki watched on with adoration, which quickly turned to horror as she realized just what was happening in her heart.

The man was quickly stealing every spare part of it.

This was bad.

Really, really bad.

When Mateo looked over to her, noticing the strained expression that was likely written all over her face, he shrugged. "You can wear that one. I have plenty more at the house."

If only that was the problem she was dealing with.

6

——————

Mateo

It was entirely possible that Mateo had bitten off more than he could chew. As more men showed up to take their place in the wranglers' cabin, he started to question if he'd hired too many.

His accountant had assured him that the business model he'd set up would allow him to hire the number of men he had before him, but now, he wasn't so sure.

It had always been just him and his siblings. Now, with all this new blood, he couldn't fight the worry that swirled within him.

He was responsible for all these people—their livelihoods were in his hands.

"Wow," Daniel grunted at his side. "I knew you'd hired twelve guys, but it seems like so much more when they're all here."

Mateo nodded, hating that Daniel had noticed the same

thing he had. This would be okay. They had enough work for the men to do. And if he had to let some of them go... well, he'd cross that bridge when the time came. "To be fair, two of these guys are helping in the kitchen... so..." He eyed his friend. "It's definitely going to be a change around here."

Daniel flashed him a smile. "I've half a mind to move in with them so I can get the full experience."

The flat look Mateo gave his friend only made Daniel laugh.

"You're right. I don't think my brother is all that thrilled about the prospect of me moving out when I get married to your cousin. I should probably make the most of the last few months I'll be at home." He clapped Mateo on the back with another grin. "We officially start training tomorrow, but I'm going to get them all together for a meeting tonight—if you want to join. We'll stay late in the cafeteria after supper."

At the mention of the mess hall, Mateo's heart stuttered. After giving Nikki a tour of her new workspace, he hadn't seen her. He couldn't decide why he felt like he was avoiding her. She was his employee. He had every right to check in on her and make sure she had everything she needed. Today she'd serve supper. It would be the first meal she would prepare for the men he was now overseeing.

And the thought of catching sight of her had his insides doing flips.

Maybe there was something wrong with him. After Caroline, he hadn't been with anyone—at least not seriously. No one had interested him in the slightest. He'd figured it was because the betrayal that Caroline had wrought had been that bad.

But now... he was wondering if it had to do with the fact that he hadn't found the right person.

Nikki could be that person.

No.

What was he thinking? She was Caroline's best friend—or she had been. But on top of that, she was his employee, *and* she had a kid! Even if he was interested, chances were slim that *she* would be. Most single moms were also single-minded... concerned mostly with taking care of their kiddos.

Daniel chuckled and nudged him, reminding him that he'd asked him something. Or he was waiting for something. "You okay, man?"

Mateo sighed. "I'm a little distracted."

"Could it be due to a certain little someone?" Daniel wagged his brows suggestively. Man, the guy had certainly come out of his shell since he'd found Aria. He was more open and social—and it had everything to do with Aria. They were meant for each other. Where one person struggled, the other excelled. He'd helped Aria learn to trust and open up again while she'd made him more confident with his friends.

Mateo didn't bother meeting the guy's eyes. "I don't know what you're talking about."

Daniel snickered. "I heard some stories about her, you know."

Stories? What kind of stories? Mateo slid his gaze to his friend but only let it linger for a moment. "Who are we talking about again?" He needed to play dumb if he wanted any chance at keeping his distance. Sophia was already planning something, and Mateo knew better than to stand in her way or try to avoid it.

His friend nudged him again. "You and I both know who I'm talking about. Sophia told Aria that Nikki is a sweetheart

—her words, not mine—and that she thinks the two of you would be a great fit."

"Yeah, well, Sophia is a romantic about everyone but herself—so I wouldn't put much stock into what she's planning."

"So, she is planning something?" Daniel drawled.

Mateo forced his expression to go blank. "I have no idea, but my sister is nothing but a meddler. If she'd been in town when you met Aria, she would have pushed you two together until your faces looked like they were smashed against a windowpane."

That had Daniel laughing. "Fair enough." They were quiet for another moment before Daniel shifted and gave Mateo a side-eyed glance once more. "What are you going to do about it?"

"What am I going to do about what?" Mateo grunted.

"Your sister pushing you and Nikki together. Do you have any inclination…"

Mateo shook his head. "None whatsoever. First and most important, she's my employee. That would be an HR nightmare."

Daniel snorted. "You're HR, so you can't use that excuse."

Choosing to ignore his friend's statement, Mateo folded his arms across his broad chest. "And we have a history."

"Wait, you do?"

He could have slugged Daniel for the third degree he was getting. "You said you heard the stories."

"Yeah, but that doesn't mean I heard about your history. I just heard about the girl who broke your heart, and she was friends—"

"That's history enough." Mateo strode away, needing to end this conversation. He didn't want to relive the past. And he had zero intention of writing a new future for himself and Nikki, so there was no reason to discuss this situation any further.

"Does that mean you're not coming to the meeting?" Daniel called out.

"I'll be there," Mateo called back. Even if it was just so he could catch a glimpse of the girl he was quickly realizing he'd become enamored with.

THE CAFETERIA SMELLED LIKE HEAVEN. The second Mateo entered the building, he had to stop to appreciate the blend of spices and herbs that she'd used in her recipe. She hadn't been lying when she'd told him that she was experienced enough to be the chef.

Two men were in the kitchen with her, looking more out of place than ducks surrounding a swan. They wore their cowboy garb, complete with their hats and boots. Their responsibilities in the kitchen would be only part of the work they'd complete while on this ranch. During the time when they weren't needed in the kitchen, they'd work to maintain the stables.

They were younger, just out of high school and definitely wet behind the ears. But they were also eager to learn.

Nikki was the last to look up when he entered the kitchen. Her eyes locked with his in a moment when the earth stopped spinning. In the corner at a small table, Paxton was working hard on a coloring book filled with horses.

The kid was made to be a cowboy. There was no doubt in Mateo's mind of that, and for some reason, it brought him joy beyond measure. Paxton didn't belong to him, and yet he couldn't shake this feeling that he was meant to be here.

Shrugging off the strange feeling, Mateo returned his focus to Nikki, but she had returned to her task at hand.

"Mark, the gravy. You have to keep stirring it until it thickens or we're going to end up with a lumpy mess. Jason, take the cornbread out of the oven. It's going to burn if we don't get it out right now." Nikki hustled toward something on the stove. She dipped a spoon into the pot and withdrew what looked like some creamy mashed potatoes. She sampled it, then reached for some salt.

She'd successfully pushed him out of her orbit without a second thought. It was actually impressive—or proof that he didn't affect her like she was affecting him.

Hmm. He had mixed feelings about that.

Without looking at him, she called out. "Is there something you need, Mr. Palmer? Or are you just curious how a kitchen works?"

He bit back a chuckle. He'd come in here with the excuse that he wanted to check on her, but deep down, he simply wanted to spend time with her. If she was any other person, he might tell her that, but this was Nikki, and something was holding him back. He needed to be professional.

Mateo shoved his hands into his pockets and rocked back on his heels. "Just making sure you have everything you need."

She paused and tossed a look in his direction. A myriad of emotions flickered on her face, after which she gave him a short nod. "I've got everything I need, thank you. Will you be staying for supper?"

He grinned, and a flirtatious comment threatened to

escape his tongue, but he refrained as he reminded himself that they weren't alone. "I wouldn't miss it."

Nikki gave him another curt nod.

Mateo wanted to stay, to linger and just spend time with her. He was tempted to move closer, to help her with the meal—any excuse to be with her. But she was busy. And clearly, she wasn't interested in his company.

He took his leave, heading out to where the rest of the men were starting to spill into the room. Most of them looked in high spirits, and a sense of comradery spread between them. But Mateo didn't have much time to survey his new employees before Jason, Mark, and Nikki exited through swinging doors with trays of food.

He found himself drawn to her as he watched her serving up the meals to the men. That smile. Those eyes. He couldn't get enough. One moment, he was leaning against the wall, watching her work. And the next, he was beside her as she motioned for her helpers to get themselves something to eat.

"You certainly look to be in your element," he whispered behind her ear, drawing a gasp from her lips. She stiffened but didn't turn to face him.

"Yeah, well, I did tell you that I was good at this sort of thing."

He moved even closer, standing directly behind her. "That you did." His voice was so low that there was no chance the people in the room could hear him. "I should have known you would be an overachiever. You were always really good at raising the bar. It was something I always admired about you." Mateo shifted until he was at her side and his arm brushed against hers.

Warmth sparked between them, sending tingles skittering along his skin until he had to stare at his arm to make sure nothing wrong was happening.

He almost missed the sharp intake of breath from her lips. Then again, maybe that had been his own. No one was looking. No one would know if he chose to go against his own better judgment and flirt with her.

But flirting seemed so shallow. Something in his head screamed that he wanted more. He wanted to know every last detail of her life.

Mateo shifted until he leaned his side against the table where they'd set up the serving trays. "You know something? I've realized I've missed you."

Her eyes rounded, then she immediately schooled her features and looked away. "I wanted to tell you something, Mateo. I need you to know that Caroline and I—"

He shook his head, which seemed to be enough to cut her off. "Tell me something I don't know about you—something new or old, I don't care. But make it something just between us."

"Just between us?" she whispered.

Mateo lifted a shoulder. This was dangerous territory, but he could pretend that it was strictly him being a good boss. "Tell me yours, and I'll tell you mine."

7

———————

Nikki

Nikki's mouth went dry. She didn't think she'd be able to speak if she tried. Her mind was whirling with various thoughts, and she couldn't keep them straight. She had the deepest desire to tell him about her falling out with Caroline—how she'd hated what her friend had done to him. She wanted Mateo to know that their friendship had crumbled shortly after their failed wedding, and yet she didn't want to admit that it had taken her so long to cut her friend out of her life.

Then there was the borderline flirty behavior she got from Mateo when people weren't nearby. She was imagining things. She had to be.

What she'd been noticing probably had everything to do with her own crush and nothing more. Mateo had always been a flirty guy. Just because he didn't have a personal space bubble didn't mean he wanted anything more from her.

The man before her was being his usual nice self. That was all.

She pushed past her disappointment. The fact that she could rationalize his behavior was more than enough to get her head on straight. Nikki frowned, though, wishing she could air out everything she needed to regarding his ex. She wanted to make it crystal clear she didn't approve of Caroline—but why was that exactly?

Because she liked his attention. That's why. Grr. She didn't *need* his attention. She needed this job.

He cleared his throat, his eyes sparkling with mischief. "How about two truths and a lie? We haven't played that game in a *long* while."

She snorted, then immediately covered her mouth with her hand, heat filling her face. Caroline had hated it when she laughed like that, and ever since she'd made fun of her all those years ago, Nikki had focused on fixing every last bit of herself that anyone might find unattractive.

But Mateo didn't appear to be bothered by her laugh. Instead, he looked amused.

Amused!

And that made her blush even worse. Was he making fun of her? She'd always been the less attractive of her little friend duo with Caroline. They were opposites in every way possible. Where Caroline was poised, blonde, thin, and had legs for days, Nikki looked like she preferred to enjoy what life had to offer in terms of sweets and other indulgences.

She wasn't *unhealthy*. Though she'd had more than one doctor tell her that she could stand to lose a few pounds.

Gah! Now she was going down the road she'd promised herself she'd steer clear from. It had taken half a decade to finally get to the point where she could be proud of who she was and every curve that came with her.

Mateo was still watching her intently, his eyes searching hers as if he could uncover every single secret she carried. Well, not today. She wasn't going to indulge him one bit.

Nikki placed a hand on her hip. "Pass."

For a moment his expression faltered. Had she hurt his feelings? Or had he finally realized that he wasn't as irresistible as he thought.

Unfortunately, he was more than irresistible. She was just lucky that they were still in a room with several other cowboys who might look their way at any moment. She wouldn't be made the fool, no matter how tempting it was to play along with Mateo's flirtatious nature.

She faced the group of men, placing her hands atop the table where the food was set out.

He did the same, and inadvertently, their fingers grazed one another.

Nikki jolted away, disbelief swirling within her as she stared down at her hand. Either the static electricity was on a different level here in this building, or something strange had just happened.

"Come on, Nikki. You're a blast from my past. Why not humor me?" Mateo said far too close to her ear.

She was tempted to shove him away from the feelings he was stirring inside her. Logic was dictating that he was only toying with her. They had nothing in common. And she knew better than to allow herself any sort of fantasy regarding him.

But her heart? That was another story.

Her heart remembered back to a time when he was sweet and friendly. How, once upon a time, he'd told Caroline to stop putting her down. Or when a bunch of jocks had gotten together with some of the cheerleaders and stolen her clothes from the locker room, Mateo had turned the tables on them, and they'd had to walk to the middle of the commons in their underwear to get their own clothes.

Those memories seemed so long ago, and Nikki had nearly forgotten all about them.

Mateo had been nothing but nice to her, and here she was, trying to keep him at arm's length for what purpose? Because of some deep-buried crush?

She sighed with a new sort of resignation. "What do you want to know?"

The light that returned to his eyes was enough to burn a hole right through to her heart. "First of all, tell me about your son."

Paxton was in the kitchen. He hadn't been interested in leaving the kitchen while she worked. The fact that Mateo was asking about him unnerved Nikki to the point that her walls came right back up into place.

"Why do you want to know about Paxton?"

Mateo shrugged, his eyes shifting to the cowboys as Daniel started leading what could only be an employee meeting. His hands were on the table again, and they were oh so close to her own. It wouldn't take any effort at all for her pinky to graze his.

She had half a mind to do just that—if only to recreate the sensation that had occurred just moments ago. Nikki was so wrapped up in trying to decide whether or not to let her fingertips graze his that she hadn't realized Mateo had been answering her question. And now he was waiting for an answer of his own. Wait a minute. He'd mentioned her ex.

Maybe he'd shifted his question because he could tell she was uncomfortable talking about her son.

Shoot! She really should have been listening.

Well, she wasn't going to make him repeat himself. That would be mortifying all on its own.

Nikki cleared her throat and gave Mateo a side-eyed glance. "There's not much to say. It wasn't a terrible relationship in the grand scheme of things."

He huffed. "That doesn't sound good either."

She shrugged. "We fell out of love." Nikki wasn't certain, but she thought she might have sensed his whole body stiffening at her confession. The embarrassment over her inability to keep a man interested was like a sour, twisting rope that knotted within her stomach and threatened to come up and out any way it could. Nikki frowned, wishing she hadn't said it.

Mateo didn't move. His eyes remained locked on Daniel where he stood.

"I mean, we were in love once. I wouldn't have married him if I hadn't been."

"But he cares for Paxton? Spends time with him?"

Her brows creased, and then she realized her mistake. Mateo thought her ex was the same man who had fathered Paxton. While Dennis had been good to Paxton, he'd never wanted to adopt him. He'd never wanted children.

Nikki swallowed hard. "Actually, his father isn't in the picture."

Mateo's head snapped around and fire filled his gaze. "What?" The single word sounded like it was spoken from something that was half-man and half-beast.

She faced him and forced a smile. "You misunderstand. My ex isn't Paxton's father. Not his biological one. Paxton knew this growing up, so when I ended things with Dennis..." She paled as she noted the confusion mixing with the irritation in his eyes. She'd always been good at reading him. Or at least she had been when they were younger.

"So, this Dennis guy... he's not related to Paxton by blood... but he was his dad, right?"

Heat rushed to her cheeks, blossoming beneath her skin. This sounded like such a mess even to her. Nikki shook her head. "Dennis never *wanted* kids. He wasn't cruel to Paxton or anything, but he never wanted to be called 'dad' either. It was like he'd put up with having one since he was part of the packaged deal."

Mateo's expression morphed into something resembling distaste. "Sure sounds like he was cruel to me. Kids don't understand the nuances of that sort of thing."

She flinched beneath the weight of his judgmental tone. "Yeah, well, he loved me, and he cared for Paxton, so that was enough..." Her argument was weak, and she was beginning to hate herself for letting Mateo get under her skin.

"So what about his father? His biological one?"

"What does it matter to you?" Nikki snapped. "He's out of the picture. A mistake in a long list of mistakes I've made in my lifetime."

His eyes softened, and he shifted closer to her. But she wasn't going to let him intimidate her. She wouldn't back away. Nikki had learned how to be strong in the face of adversity. And this situation was no different.

He lifted a hand slightly, and for a moment she imagined that he was going to reach out and caress her face. The way he was looking at her—Goodness... No. She couldn't go there. Nikki schooled her features in an attempt to recover the bantering tone they'd had. "Your turn."

Mateo's hand dropped to his side. That easy smile returned as if their conversation had never happened. "What about me?"

"What have you been up to?" She'd noted that he didn't wear a ring, but in his line of work, she wouldn't be surprised if he chose not to for safety reasons. She figured he wasn't married, but he could be dating someone. If he was, she couldn't imagine anyone approving of him shamelessly flirting with her.

It would be best to get to the bottom of it now so she could kick her desire for him once and for all.

"Are you wanting to know about my exes? Because I don't have a kid."

She scoffed. "You're the one who chose that line of questioning. It's only fair you continue it."

His grin was almost a wicked one. "Okay. No kids. No marriages failed or otherwise. I only came close that one time, and up until recently, I had no intention of going down that path again. Is that enough information for you?"

"Until recently? What changed?" She only realized she'd spoken the question aloud when he ended up answering it.

"Because up until now, I haven't noticed anyone who is worth risking my heart for."

Something weird was taking place in her stomach, consuming the sour and bitter mixture there and replacing it with a jittery, floaty feeling. He wasn't talking about her, was he?

There was no way she was going to ask him. Talk about embarrassing.

She lifted her chin as if in defiance. "Good luck with that."

He inched closer still, his voice lowering until it held a husky quality to it. "What about you? Any prospects?"

Nikki barked out a laugh. "Prospects? You mean, have I met anyone I'd jump into the fire for after dealing with my husband falling for someone else and telling me I no longer interested him?" She knew she shouldn't be directing her anger at Mateo. None of this was his fault. He was just her boss. She should be falling at his feet and thanking him for helping her. And yet, she couldn't keep the venom from her voice.

Unexpectedly, his alluring grin faltered, and he frowned at her.

"To answer your question. No. And I have zero intention of seeking anything out." She turned to leave him, but his hand wrapped around her wrist, immobilizing her with his touch. Nikki stared down at where he touched her, and she froze as the warmth from his touch seeped deep into her bones.

"Nikki—" he whispered.

"Mateo, you have anything else to add?" Daniel's voice called, and Mateo released her as if he'd been burned. He glanced over to the men, and she chose that moment to escape him.

The whole situation was weird, and she needed to clear her head before she let any wayward thoughts take over—more specifically, thoughts of Mateo being anything more than an old friend.

8

─────────

Mateo

M ateo couldn't stop thinking about the conversation he'd had with Nikki on that first night. He'd made a couple attempts to speak to her again over the next week so they could clear the air, but every chance he got was thwarted.

Sometimes, she slipped away like she had that night. Other times, they were interrupted by Mark or Jason. And occasionally, Daniel—who couldn't read the room.

Nikki's ex was an idiot. How could any man not see the treasure they had in a woman like her? These days, most of the women Mateo had come across were vapid more often than not. People were judgmental and conceited. They married for two reasons—money or a trophy.

Caroline had proved that to him from the beginning; he just hadn't realized it until it was too late. She had actually done him the best favor by failing to show up for their wedding ceremony. Good people were hard to find and even harder to keep. Whoever this Dennis guy was, he didn't deserve Nikki.

And you do? the voice in his head seemed to ask.

Mateo pushed that thought away as quickly as it had come. As far as Nikki was concerned, she could be his friend —she was his friend. And he didn't want her thinking that she was worth less just because some guy didn't want to stay with her.

Two guys, he reminded himself. Idiots. The both of them.

He stood in the back of the cafeteria at breakfast, watching the men that Daniel oversaw eat their first meal of the day. He was determined to speak to her, and the only way he saw that happening was if he started eating some of his meals here with the other men in his employ. Sophia seemed to be the only one who noticed that he had been missing from the occasional meal with the family, but she'd been smart enough not to mention it outright.

Daniel was the last to arrive, and he stopped short as he entered the building. "What are you doing here? I thought you were going to be taking a drive to the city first thing this morning."

That had been something on his list, but he'd opted to postpone it. The supplies he needed in the city weren't going anywhere.

He flashed Daniel a smile. "I wanted to eat breakfast with you—touch base on how your side of things is going. Seeing as you usually eat dinner with Aria and breakfast with your family..." Mateo wasn't going to admit he'd overheard Daniel telling some of the guys that he'd be here before breakfast ended so they could get an early start on herding some of their sheep to one of the Callahan pastures. They were also doing a trade. Mateo needed a good, strong bull for his cows, and Zeke was interested in adding to his livestock.

Daniel appeared confused for all of a second before his eyes darted to the swinging doors that led to the kitchen. Then a smile stretched across his face. "I have a feeling that this has more to do with you seeing a certain someone."

Mateo rolled his eyes. "If I wanted to see a *certain someone*, I would just pull her aside and talk to her."

"So why aren't you doing that?"

Because if he pulled her aside to talk to her in an *official* capacity, he didn't think it would be appropriate to tell her that the men in her life were jerks and she was better off without them. But if she managed to walk past him and he could strike up a conversation, then that would be a different matter altogether.

Daniel didn't need to know any of that.

Mateo ran a hand down his face. "What's the plan with the sheep? I know you wanted to transport them in trailers, but since we couldn't acquire them, the job is going to be more difficult."

"It's nothing I can't handle," Daniel said, moving farther into the room toward the table where most of the food had already been set out. Good. He could tell when his choice in conversation was being forcibly changed.

There were a lot of things Mateo liked about Daniel, but his ability to move on to something else was one of the best.

They dished up some breakfast, and Mateo chose a table closest to the kitchen in case Nikki made an appearance. He needed to talk to her.

That's not true, and you know it, that little voice chided. *Besides, Nikki doesn't want to speak to you. If she did, she'd be easier to nail down.*

Mateo's focus drifted from the kitchen doors to the man seated across from him. He found Daniel smirking like he knew a secret and was about to crow it to the whole world. "You like her."

"What?" Mateo scoffed.

"How long?"

"What do you mean, how long?"

Daniel leaned forward, and his voice lowered. "Come on, man. You can't tell me that you don't. You literally moved her into your home."

"She has her own space. It's upstairs, and my room is downstairs. It's hardly inappropriate," Mateo insisted a little *too* defensively.

"It's okay that you do. Even Sophia thinks so. But you have to tell me how long it's been going on."

Mateo didn't think it was possible, but Daniel looked even more like he was conspiring with someone. It was near impossible to hear his next words over the hum of voices in the cafeteria.

"Were you two already talking before she came here? I won't breathe a word to anyone."

Scowling, Mateo leaned forward so his face was far too close to his friend's. "I don't know what Sophia has told you, but you've got it all wrong. I assure you. Nothing is going on with me and her. And I don't have feelings for her, alright?"

"Who says you have feelings? I want to know about your crush."

Mateo raised his hands into the air with exasperation. "I don't have a crush on her," he said a little too loudly—okay, far too loudly.

The quiet hum of voices abruptly died down. Mateo glanced around to find most of the men in the room looking their way. Worse than that, the object of his interest stood on just this side of the swinging kitchen doors with a platter in hand and her focus locked on him. The expression she wore was completely unreadable.

Did she know that he was talking about her? He sure hoped not. That wouldn't go over well at all.

Whirling back to Daniel, Mateo wasn't surprised to find that his friend was laughing quietly under his breath. Mateo pointed an accusatory finger at him. "You and your fiancée and my sister need to stop gossiping about stuff you know nothing about." He pushed away from the table and shot to his feet.

Without really knowing what he planned on doing, he headed for the kitchen.

Nikki had disappeared behind those doors. And while he knew it was unwise to go seeking her out after his little outburst, he couldn't bring himself to care.

He pushed through the swinging doors and plastered the smile he was so used to wearing onto his face. "Hello, Nikki," he drawled.

She looked up from where she stood at the sink, rinsing bowls from what had likely held pancake batter. "Is there something you need, Mr. Palmer?"

Why did he suddenly hate the way she said his name like that? Mateo fought the urge to drag a hand through his hair and insist she call him by his first name. That wouldn't be wise at all.

"I was wondering if you needed anything from the city. You mentioned that you'd be putting a list of supplies together. Now that you've been here for a week—"

Her expression brightened, and he found himself wanting to be the sole person who could do that to her.

"Actually, yes." She pulled back from the sink and wiped her hands on her aprons. "I have a list of things we need, but I'll need to go with you. How long do you plan on being in the city? Do I have time to put together a quick lunch for the guys? Or will we be back in time?"

"There's a chance we could get back in time, but that depends on you."

She frowned.

"Your list. How big are we talking here?"

She smiled, and it felt like she could light the whole earth with it. "I already did some research. There's a restaurant supply store in Colorado Springs that should have most, if not all, of the stuff I need. After that we can get the fresh produce from the local markets here."

"Then I don't see why we couldn't make it back for a late lunch."

"But Mom, I thought today you said you'd let me see some of the horses." A small voice came from the corner of the room, and Mateo shifted his attention to the source. Paxton stood, frowning, his colored pictures in his hands.

Nikki gave him an apologetic smile. "I know, sweetie, but we talked about what it means for us to be here. This is my job—"

Mateo moved past Nikki to crouch down in front of the boy like he had that first day they'd arrived. "Have you ever ridden a horse?"

Paxton shook his head, and Mateo fought the instinct to shoot his mother a surprised look. But he had to remind himself that, up until recently, she'd been living in the city. Why would she have any reason to take the kid riding?

He grinned at the boy and chucked him under the chin. "I'll tell you what. After these errands, I'm more or less free today. I'll take you to meet all the horses you want. Then maybe, if your mother is okay with it, we can go riding. How does that sound?"

"But he doesn't know—" Nikki started to argue, but Mateo cut her off.

"Anyone living on a ranch should know the basics about riding and controlling a horse. As Paxton is currently a resident, it'd be my pleasure to teach him a thing or two about riding."

Nikki's hesitation cut at Mateo. Was she actually worried that he wouldn't take care of her boy? Or was this something else? Her eyes found his, delving deeper, stirring a vulnerability within him. "I'm really busy, Mateo. I can't be there to supervise."

"Who said anything about you supervising? The kid can't spend his last summer before kindergarten holed away in a kitchen coloring pictures. He should be out there in the world getting scraped up and learning what it means to be a cowboy."

Pure and utter excitement filled the boy's features. He looked up at his mother with a wistful kind of longing, and Nikki was clearly losing her will to fight him on this. When she heaved a sigh, both Mateo and Paxton grinned like they'd just won the lottery.

Mateo turned to Paxton and offered his fist. The kid bumped his against Mateo's, and there was no missing the smile that tugged at the corners of Nikki's lips.

Winning.

9

———————

Nikki

$\mathcal{W}$hile they were in front of her son, Mateo was all professional. Well, except for when he got all buddy-buddy with Paxton.

Nikki couldn't drag her eyes away from them when that happened. The whole trip to the city and back, Mateo acted like the same guy she'd gotten to know a decade ago. He was all charm and smiles—and she wanted to hate it, but she couldn't deny how good it felt to have the attention of a man like him, even if it wasn't for romantic reasons.

She'd finished up a simple lunch for the men and wandered out to the corral where Mateo was yet again down on eye level with her son as he discussed the rules for riding. She couldn't hear what Mateo was saying as his voice was too low, but based on how Paxton was drinking in every single word, she knew it was good.

Paxton nodded, and Mateo grinned at him. He was so

good with her son that it made her heart twist in her chest. He would have been such a good father. It was a shame he'd never settled down with anyone after Caroline.

Mateo glanced in her direction, and their eyes locked. She stiffened under his stare. It didn't matter how many times he looked at her like that; she couldn't shake the way it sent goosebumps rippling beneath her skin.

In that second, time stood still. There was no other way to describe it. She couldn't move, and all she thought about was the idea that he saw something special in her. Nikki couldn't recall the last time someone looked at her like that.

No matter how much she tried to convince herself that there was nothing between them, in this moment, her heart refused to accept it.

Someone nudged her, and Nikki gasped as she turned to find Sophia standing beside her at the corral, watching Paxton's riding lesson. She smiled serenely as she folded her arms atop the wooden fence pole. "Your kid is adorable," Sophia said.

Nikki forced herself to drag her attention back to the duo and found Mateo had turned his back to them. Paxton was staring up at the saddle like it was his very own Mount Everest. Mateo's robust chuckle echoed toward them at something her son had said. "Thanks," Nikki said.

"He's a real sweetheart, too."

Nikki swiveled her attention to Mateo's sister and regarded her with curiosity. When had Sophia interacted with her son? Sure, they were all staying under the same roof, but Nikki had tried her hardest to make sure that they stayed out of everyone's way. She didn't want anyone to complain about her presence, and she'd told Paxton as much. They had a good thing going for them in the larger bedroom. She didn't want to lose it.

Sophia chuckled and turned to face Nikki. Her eyes trailed over Nikki from head to toe, assessing, and Nikki stiffened. Sophia didn't seem like the type of person to be judgmental when it came to looks. She had her own set of curves. Though to Nikki, Sophia pulled them off far better than anyone she knew. It came with her ancestry. The woman was made to dance a salsa with some handsome man in a tux.

Shifting uncomfortably, Nikki forced her eyes away from Sophia and nodded toward Mateo. "I never knew how good he was with kids. Did you?" She could feel Sophia's eyes on her, drilling heat into the side of her face before she turned away from Nikki and watched what was going on.

Mateo had lifted Paxton onto the saddle, and he was talking earnestly to him. Based on Paxton's pale skin, he wasn't thrilled with how high up off the ground he was.

Sophia offered a small smile. "Yeah, I knew. Mateo loves kids. Always has. I think it came with his love of dogs. He's always been a sucker for that sort of thing, and he's had to fight off women left and right because of it."

Of course, he did. There was nothing more attractive than a man who loved kids and dogs. Nikki knew it, and so did every other woman on the planet. She burned with questions. Why hadn't Mateo settled down? Surely there were plenty of women to choose from. He could have literally anyone.

But Nikki kept her mouth clamped shut. Mateo was still her boss. She couldn't afford for Sophia to notice she had feelings for him. Too complicated.

"Caroline ruined him." Sophia said it so quietly and so

full of bitterness that Nikki wasn't sure she'd heard her correctly.

"I'm sorry?" she asked.

Sophia turned a sour stare on Nikki, but it wasn't really directed at her. It was more out of solidarity than anything else—a support for her brother. "She broke him. After he found out that she cheated on him and left with that guy, he swore he wasn't going to date forever. It took a couple years for me to convince him to go on a date with no strings attached. Slowly, he's gotten back out there, but he's refused to get serious."

Nikki breathed out a surprised breath. "Wow. I mean... I don't blame him... but..."

"Yeah," Sophia muttered. "He was so excited to move on to that married stage of his life. He kept talking about how he planned on starting a family right away and—" Sophia cut herself off, snapping her mouth shut before she met Nikki's eyes again. "It's just too bad, you know?"

Nodding wordlessly, Nikki glanced over to where Mateo was joking around with Paxton. There was color back in his cheeks. It was good for him to try something new, and she had a sinking feeling that if it had been anyone besides Mateo, Paxton wouldn't have taken to it. Mateo was cut from a different cloth. He had a way of drawing people in and making them feel like they were priceless.

A lump formed in her throat and the all too familiar guilt returned to her gut. She slid her gaze to Sophia and sucked in sharply when she noticed Sophia staring at her. Nikki wrung her hands and forced her voice to be stronger than she felt like giving. "I tried to tell him—Mateo—that I didn't agree with what Caroline did. I mean, who would? It was awful. I still can't believe she'd risk everything..." She shook her head, feeling sick all over.

The truth of the matter was that she'd stayed friends with Caroline for a couple of years after that experience—and hated herself for it.

Mateo hadn't deserved that treatment. No one did, but especially not Mateo.

The man was hot. But more than his looks, he was beautiful on the inside. He should have had everything good in life. Karma had practically demanded it... and yet Caroline had come into his life and shattered that good heart of his.

"I'm not friends with her now," Nikki whispered. "I haven't heard from her in years."

"Good." Sophia's sharp tone would have made Nikki flinch if she was any other person in the world. She had every right to be protective of her brother, and Nikki found she could appreciate her desire to be just that.

Nikki offered Sophia a small smile.

Sophia returned it in kind before facing her brother. "I'm not going to judge you for your friendships. I wanted you to know that." She glanced at Nikki out of the corner of her eye. "I'm happy you cut loose the dead weight. You were always too good of a friend to Caroline. She didn't deserve someone who was as loyal as you."

Nikki's brows lifted. "What makes you think I was loyal?"

The woman scoffed, and the sound was followed quickly after with a laugh. "I might not have been in the same grade as you and Mateo, but I spent my share of time hovering in the background whenever you guys came here to hang out. I noticed things. Caroline was a brat with a capital B. You were too good of a friend for someone like that. I always thought that Mateo should have dated you instead of Caroline."

There was no stifling the sharp intake of breath that ended with Nikki all but choking on her own spittle. She gaped wide-eyed at Sophia, wondering if she'd said as much to her brother.

Worse still, had Mateo said something in response to that sort of statement?

Her legs shook, and she reached out to hold onto the corral with one hand to steady herself. There was absolutely no way she'd ask. She couldn't afford to add fuel to the fire.

She couldn't help but wonder if Sophia was fishing for information. Or maybe it was just wishful thinking. If Mateo had sent his sister to find out about Nikki's feelings, would Nikki finally be able to admit she held some attraction for her cowboy boss?

Sophia laughed. "I take it that you don't agree."

Nikki blinked several times and forced herself to shake her head. "No. I mean, sure... but..." Her face burned, and she fought to find the words that would get her out of this blustering mess. "What I meant to say was that I hadn't really thought about it."

Liar.

Sophia didn't look convinced, and why would she? Based on the way that Nikki had just reacted to her statement, there was no reason for her to believe her. And now she'd likely go off and prattle on about her findings to her brother.

Nikki's hand reached out and landed on Sophia's arm. "I know what you're thinking, but don't."

One side of Sophia's mouth quirked upward. "And what exactly is that?"

"That you think I'm attracted to your brother."

"And you're not?"

Just like that, the heat intensified tenfold in her face. "Of course, he's attractive. Someone would have to be blind not to see that. He's definitely good-looking, but not in the way you think. He's..." She was desperate. This was so embarrassing! "He's my boss, Sophia. Nothing more. I would never act on any kind of attraction I may or may not have for someone who is signing my paycheck. So please... don't make this out to be something it's not."

Sophia cocked her head like the pleased predator she was. Then she shrugged. "Okay. I won't say anything." She practically beamed at Nikki. "On one condition."

All relief that Nikki had temporarily experienced went up in smoke.

"If Mateo asks you out, you accept."

"What? I can't—"

"You know what I think? I think the two of you would be good for each other. More than you probably realize." With that, she hurried away—far too quickly for Nikki to make any semblance of an argument to the contrary.

Nikki stared after her, half tempted to chase her down and tell her she was crazy and half determined to stay where she was with her feet planted. Who was she to argue with something that sounded so... right?

Slowly, she turned around and watched Mateo with her son. Her eyes locked with Mateo's several other times before she had to excuse herself to start making dinner. She was certain she'd hear all about their lesson from Paxton when she prepared to put him to bed this evening.

Her heart fluttered as she went over the conversation she'd had with Mateo's sister.

If anything, she felt a little less crazy about her growing feelings for her boss.

10

———

Mateo

It had been two weeks since Nikki started working at Winding Creek Ranch. Two whole weeks of Mateo dancing around any interaction he had with the woman who was quickly garnering his complete attention.

He couldn't stop thinking about her—about the fact that she was staying in his home just upstairs.

It was dark outside, and most everyone had gone to bed. But he could hear quiet footsteps overhead, and he knew she wasn't asleep yet. That was something he'd discovered early on. Nikki was more restless than the average person, and perhaps that had more to do with her being a mother than anything else.

Mateo rested on his bed, staring up at the ceiling as if doing so would give him the power to see her through the plaster and paint. Of course, it wouldn't. That would be highly inappropriate.

He had half a mind to go up there, knock on her door, and just talk to her. How would she react? Would she brush him off and tell him to leave her alone?

Hopefully not.

Mateo was already getting to his feet when he paused at the sound of the footsteps heading from her room down the hall. His ears strained as he wondered if she was going to the restroom or if she was coming down the stairs.

Moving to his bedroom door, he pulled it open a crack and listened to the quiet house.

When the creaking sound of the stairs reached him, a grin spread across his face. She was coming downstairs for something. Now would be the perfect opportunity to seek her out.

He hurried with quiet steps toward the kitchen. The only reason to come downstairs would be to get something from that room. A drink? A snack?

Mateo made it to the kitchen only seconds before Nikki arrived. He'd managed to get a glass in his hand and position himself leaning against the counter in the most nonchalant way he could when she stopped in the doorway with a gasp.

"I'm so sorry," she let out breathily, quickly backing up a few steps.

He straightened. "Don't leave on account of me."

She stopped.

Thank heavens she stopped.

Nikki glanced around the darkened kitchen, lit only by the light beneath the microwave. "Why are you up?"

He lifted his glass as if that were answer enough. She'd never know that she was the reason for his restless nights as of late.

Her eyes snagged on the glass, and he could have sworn

that she blushed when she realized her question hadn't been necessary. Of course, it was too dark to say for sure, but he imagined it all the same.

"You?" he asked.

She inched into the kitchen and gave him a timid smile, which made her appear even more beautiful. He let his attention sweep over her from the messy bun atop her head to the white tank she wore paired with pajama pants. Her feet were bare, and he couldn't help imagining a possible future where she was so comfortable in his home that this became a common occurrence.

"Same," she whispered, reminding him that he'd asked her a question. "May I?" She gestured toward him as she drew nearer.

The temptation to stay put had him stiffening where he stood. The cupboard with the glasses was directly behind him. She'd have to lean around him to get a cup for some water. He'd be able to smell the floral scent of her shampoo.

She stopped a few feet short of him, hesitating when he didn't move.

One side of his mouth quirked upward, and he took a small step to the side to grant her access. It wasn't so much that he would miss out on that smell he craved, but it was enough to allow her to get what she came for.

"How are you liking the job?" he asked before lifting his glass to his lips. "Is it everything you ever dreamed of?" He was teasing her, his tone making that perfectly apparent.

Nikki glanced at him out of the corner of her eye, the smile tugging at her lips making his heart sing. "Actually, it is."

His brows lifted with interest. "Really?"

She nodded, honesty easily readable in her gaze. "Do

you know how nice it is to have the freedom to run my own kitchen? I don't really have to report to anyone—well, except you."

"I can see the appeal," he said. His eyes followed her as she put the glass beneath the faucet and filled it with water. Half expecting her to take her glass and escape, he was pleasantly surprised when she remained in the kitchen and took a place a few feet away from him.

Nikki had one hand wrapped around her waist as she held the glass with the other. She watched him over the brim of her glass. "How do you feel everything is going with your expansion? Is it everything you hoped for?"

Mateo cocked his head. No one had asked him that yet. His siblings just went along with what he told them was going to happen. Not even Sophia had any disagreements. They were all happy. Daniel was his employee, and he was doing an amazing job in his position. But no one had asked him if he was happy with the changes. "I'm happy," he replied.

"That's good. It's quite an accomplishment—what you're working to do here. Expansion is always hard."

"It is," he agreed.

She took a sip of her water and placed the cup on the counter. "Paxton can't stop talking about his riding lessons."

A grin spread across Mateo's face. "He's an amazing kid. A natural, too. Seems like he was born to be a cowboy. Did you know that?"

She laughed. "You're sweet."

"No, I'm honest. Did you know that he's already figuring out how to get into the saddle on his own?"

By the look of surprise that flickered in her gaze, it was clear that Paxton hadn't told his mother that tidbit of information. After that first lesson, she hadn't been able to observe for more than a few minutes, so everything she'd know would be straight from the horse's mouth.

Nikki shook her head. "I know he said you were proud of him for helping to brush his horse down after the ride. He's fascinated with what's needed to take care of horses. I know it's only a matter of time before he begs me to get him one."

Mateo chuckled. "I remember feeling that way when I was a kid. I think it comes with the territory of having parents who work on a ranch."

"Yeah, well, it might just be the end of me. I can barely pay to keep a roof over my head. There's no way I can afford to keep a roof over the head of a horse, too."

Her words struck a chord within him. When she arrived, she seemed nervous—but not desperate for the job. Every so often, she let something slip that made him wonder just how bad things were for her.

Nikki let out a strangled laugh, but he didn't laugh with her. He wanted to help her.

"You could keep a horse here. At the ranch. Even if you get a job somewhere else and move on..." He hated that idea —not the helping her part—the her moving on part. He didn't like the idea of her leaving. And he definitely didn't like the idea of her finding someone else to be in her life.

Her mouth fell open as she gazed at him. He could have laughed at her shock, but he kept his expression serious. He had been, after all.

"I couldn't do that," she finally whispered.

"Sure you could. It's not like we don't have the space." Mateo shrugged. It wasn't a big deal. In the grand scheme of things, what was one more horse? Besides, he'd been honest when he said the kid was a natural. One day, that kid could oversee a bunch of wranglers just like Daniel was doing for him.

Nikki looked away as she reached for her glass and brought it to her lips. He could see the hesitancy in her gaze—or rather, in the way she didn't meet his eyes. A smile tugged at her mouth, but it didn't seem to brighten her countenance at all. "I'll think about it," she said.

"You'll do more than think about it." Mateo winked. "One of these days, you won't be able to resist."

"Is that so?" she mused. "Like the way girls can't resist you?"

Her words caught him off guard. If he wasn't leaning back against the counter, he might have stumbled back a step. Mateo wagged his brows at her, pleased that she seemed to be willing to play along.

Mateo leaned closer and lowered his voice. "You're absolutely right. I'm utterly irresistible. It's about time that you figured that out."

"Oh, I figured it out a long time ago."

He laughed. "Do tell."

She cocked her head, not backing up from him like he'd expected her to. To his surprise, she drew a line down the middle of his chest. "You remember in high school... when we were in the same home economics class?"

"Yeah?" he drawled, inching closer. His eyes snagged on her lips. He could only imagine the feeling of her lips on his.

Her lips quirked upward—the only indication that she was about to rip his heart out of his chest in the next second. "Who could forget the first day when we were making pudding?" She snickered. "And when you spilled the entire jug of milk all over the counter, your shirt, your shoes, and the teacher standing next to you during the demonstration?"

Mateo frowned as she let out a laugh and moved away from him. That wasn't one of his better moments. What was she talking about? Out of every memory in high school, she chose that.

He thought about matching her steps and going after her, but at that moment, Sophia entered the kitchen. She glanced from him to Nikki, then back. A knowing grin spread across her face that not even his warning scowl could wipe away.

Unfortunately, she didn't seem to like the way he was looking at her because she folded her arms and asked, "Did you call Annie back? She left you another message today. She said you still owe her a second date."

Mateo didn't have to look in Nikki's direction to know she'd grown uncomfortable by this change in subject matter. She shifted from one foot to the other several times, and the air felt cooler. "No," he ground out.

"Why not?" Sophia asked, her voice sounding more innocent than she really was. He knew what she was doing. This was manipulation at its finest.

Nikki murmured something about being tired before he could answer.

But Sophia stepped in her path. "Hey, Nikki. Have you heard about the country club on the outskirts of town?"

Nikki glanced from Sophia to Mateo. "I haven't."

"Well, you should go tonight. It would be nice for you to get out and have some fun. I'm sure Mateo could take you if you want to carpool. He goes there at least twice a month."

"Oh..." Once again, her eyes found his. "Unfortunately, I don't think I'll be able to go. I'm pretty busy."

"Don't be ridiculous. Mateo is your boss. I'm sure he'd give you one night off." Sophia lifted her eyebrows expectantly, but Mateo couldn't speak. What was she up to? First, she brought up Annie. Now she was trying to set him up with Nikki?

"Well, I don't have a sitter—"

"Let me watch him. He's such a cutie. I bet we could have a lot of fun together."

Mateo waited, holding his breath. Was this actually going to work?

Nikki shook her head. "I couldn't ask you to do—"

"If this is about having someone to go with, I can ask my cousin Aria. She's great with kids. And so is Daniel. They could tag team it since they're hanging out tonight anyway." Sophia moved closer, giving Nikki her best puppy dog eyes.

This couldn't possibly work.

11

____

Nikki

Nikki could feel her resolve waning. She had to admit that going out for the evening sounded really nice. She hadn't had a chance to just let loose in a very long time. After having Paxton, she'd spent a lot of her time focused on being a mother. He had become her whole world. Even after she'd met Dennis, she'd continued with the status quo.

Dennis would take her out, but he was the one who planned their outings. He'd picked what they did and when. She didn't fault him. On the contrary, she'd been the sort of person who was happy to let her husband choose what they did. He made the money. He liked to take charge, and it was a way for her to show him how much she cared for him.

Now, Sophia was presenting her with endless possibilities. What if she didn't want to go to the country club?

Sophia would probably tell her that everyone needed a night out once in a while—that was who she was.

Who was Nikki kidding? She wanted to go out dancing. She loved dancing when she was younger. So why was she hesitating?

Nikki's eyes shifted to Mateo. She couldn't read his expression no matter how much she wanted to. How would he feel if she accepted Sophia's offer? Her eyes locked with his. "I wouldn't want to put you out—"

"It's no trouble," Mateo said, almost too quickly.

She bit back a smile. "Are you sure?" Her question was to both of them this time. The last thing she wanted was for either of them to resent her for needing their help.

"Of course."

"Absolutely,"

They spoke at once, dredging a small laugh from Nikki's throat.

Sophia went on. "Aria loves kids. So does Daniel. They'll make sure Paxton doesn't even miss you."

Nikki nodded. It was easier to agree knowing that Sophia would be coming along with them. "Then I guess there's nothing more to discuss. I'd love to go see what this country club has to offer."

"It's a date!" Sophia blurted, earning a sharp look from her brother—one that Nikki didn't miss. He didn't want this to be a date, and she couldn't figure out why that made a flicker of disappointment bloom in her chest.

She didn't want to go on a date with her boss either—but the boy she'd known in high school? The boy she'd had a crush on all those years ago? There was a little girl in her heart who wanted to take advantage of the fairytale, no matter how wrong it was—no matter how unbelievable.

And that was exactly what this was—unbelievable.

She'd foolishly allowed herself to believe that he might like her more than as just an employee—as more than just an acquaintance. Her embarrassment only continued to drag her down as she sat beside him in the truck on the way to the country club. Rubbing the hem of her shirt between her finger and thumb, she forced herself to push aside all the buried feelings she had for Mateo.

He'd practically been manipulated into taking her this evening by his sister, just like Nikki felt she'd been manipulated into coming. It was a stretch, but if anything could occur from spending time at the same location with him that wasn't her workplace, it might be possible to rekindle the friendship they once had.

Nikki nodded sharply as if the movement alone would be enough to get into the right headspace.

Friends. That was all this would ever be.

She turned her head to look out the window, and the ride remained quietly uncomfortable. She itched to get out of her seat and expend some of this nervous energy. The second the truck pulled to a stop before a beautiful building where throngs of people were heading inside and out, she launched herself from the confines of the vehicle and shut the door with a final snap of her wrist. Sophia was at her side in an instant, grinning like she'd won the lottery. Her excitement was infectious, and it allowed Nikki to ignore the swirling, tumultuous feelings that threatened to overflow within her.

Sophia linked her arm through Nikki's and practically dragged her toward the club. "This place isn't like anything you've ever experienced. There are no membership fees for dance nights or dining at the restaurant. All the profit they make is put into their equine therapy services. The guy who owns the place is practically a saint, and he's completely loaded."

Nikki raised her brows and glanced around at the place the second they crossed the threshold. Right off the entrance was a space dedicated to the dance nights. Tables and chairs lined the edges of the room, and on one side a bartender served drinks. Everything from the immaculate wood floors to the decorative lighting made it clear this place had been designed to impress. And yet, there was no feeling as though one didn't belong here.

Those in attendance were dressed in everything from jeans and fitted t-shirts to dresses and button-downs with ties. Music played over the speakers, and it looked as though a DJ was the one choosing the tunes.

Chatter hummed all around her. She'd never been to a place quite like this one.

"Pretty cool, huh?" Mateo's voice grazed her ear to her left, and she jumped at his closeness. His warm body brushed against her arm, sending waves of goosebumps scattering across her skin. It wasn't even cold, and yet she couldn't shake the chill that wracked her body.

Before she could answer, a squeal erupted from the crowd.

"Mateo! I didn't think you'd come!"

It only took a moment for Mateo to shoot a threatening look at his sister for Nikki to understand what Sophia had done. She'd planned this whole thing. In order to get Mateo to come, she'd dragged Nikki into it.

On the one hand, it was nice to know that Mateo was willing to drive them here for Nikki's benefit—as he was making it clear they were still friends. But on the other hand? Sophia wasn't trying to set the two of them up. Nope. She'd made some sort of agreement to bring Mateo here for that woman's benefit.

She was tall—with legs for days. Curves in all the right places, making her appear as though she was the true embodiment of an hourglass. She had the most perfect complexion—ivory skin with just the right amount of blush across her cheeks. Freckles dotted her nose and the soft rosy coloring. Her hair was a pale strawberry blonde, and she turned heads as she came rushing forward.

This woman drew the focus from both men and women as she moved through the crowd. Of course, she was interested in Mateo. Like found like. They were practically made for each other. If they got together, their babies would be the most beautiful beings on the planet.

She didn't bother looking Nikki's way as she threw her arms around Mateo. She lingered in his arms before pulling back and placing a hand on his cheek. "You owe me your first dance, you scoundrel. I've been trying to reach you for days."

"I've been busy," Mateo said in a flat tone.

Nikki felt like she was watching something she had no right to. These two needed their space. As carefully as she could, she slipped away. Thankfully, Sophia came with her —though her companionship didn't last long.

Nikki should have left a half hour ago. Sophia was chatting with the woman who had stolen Mateo's first dance. She'd been the woman Sophia had mentioned before they came. They were laughing and joking around like they were best of friends while Nikki had morphed into a wallflower.

Her stomach churned, and as she watched several people who were ten times as good-looking as herself, she felt even more out of place. She didn't belong here—that much was clear. The only problem was that Mateo had been their driver. Maybe she could find someone to take pity on her and take her home. Or perhaps she could call Daniel and he could come get her.

She moved toward the door, sending one more glance around the room, but Mateo wasn't in sight. Good. He wouldn't want her slipping out without telling them. She'd send Sophia a text. That would be enough.

Just as she was about to reach the door, an arm slipped around her middle and she was tugged toward the dance floor just as a slow song began.

Her breath snagged in her throat. Her heart exploded against her ribs. And the familiar scent of his aftershave permeated the air between them.

"Where do you think you're going?" Mateo said, his voice low. His eyes flashed with amusement... and something else. They were pressed against each other as he spun her around the dance floor. She could barely breathe, and it had every-thing to do with the fire his touch elicited against her skin.

"I was just... I thought I should... I'm tired." It was the only thing that would make sense. "And Paxton probably needs me."

He chuckled, the sound warm and inviting and all too close. "We haven't even been here a whole hour."

"Exactly," she said breathlessly, "I haven't been away from him this long before."

Mateo's eyes locked on hers in a stare that was all too

intimate for her liking. "Then I suppose it's a good thing I caught you before you slipped away." His hold on her tightened, and her breath hitched.

Too close.

Too *close*.

Her thoughts were running away from her. She couldn't allow herself to believe this was anything more than friendship. Mateo was a flirt. She'd known that from the start. She needed to get her head cleared and locked down before he did some real damage.

Their dance ended, and he carted her off toward the back doors. The air was cooler out on the balcony than it was on the dance floor, and it allowed Nikki to breathe easier. Mateo stood beside her, his arm brushing against hers as they both leaned against the railing and looked out at the endless property before them.

Mateo was quiet for a long moment, then he sighed. "After Caroline, I forced myself to close off to everyone else."

She stiffened. Was he actually talking about Caroline now? He'd avoided this conversation from the get-go. What was happening?

He cleared his throat but didn't face her. "She really did a number on me. I couldn't even bring myself to say her name —that was how bad it was. And trying to trust anyone with my heart? Fat chance." He shook his head before running a hand through his hair. "But I suppose that's to be expected, right?" This time he turned his eyes toward her, his gaze pleading. It was as if he needed her to give him permission to be vulnerable.

"Of course, it's to be expected," she whispered. "You gave your heart to her, and she ripped it out of your chest. If anyone faults you for being hesitant to find love again, they're crazy."

A small smile tugged at the corner of his lips. "I think the statute of limitations to blame my trust issues on my failed relationship expired several years ago."

She shrugged. "I don't know. Some scars run deeper than we realize."

He shifted beside her before turning an imploring stare on her. "You sound like you speak from experience."

Nikki failed miserably at keeping her blush contained. There was no way she would be able to ignore his statement. Already she could feel her ability to keep her own secrets in check. There was no way to pull her gaze from his, and the longer he stared at her, the harder it became to keep her mouth shut. "Paxton's father—he wasn't the kindest man."

Mateo scowled as if he could do something about what she'd confessed, but there was no way. She hadn't heard from him in years. Their marriage had been quick, and they'd gotten pregnant shortly after. But as soon as she found out she was expecting, his demeanor changed.

She swallowed back the bile that the bad memories dredged up. "Let's just say he didn't hold back when he wanted to put me in my place."

"Did he hurt you?" Mateo snarled.

Her eyes flew wide. "What? No. Well, not physically, at least. But words can cut just as deep." This was so embarrassing. She couldn't believe she'd stayed with him as long as she had. Thankfully, he hadn't fought her on ending their relationship. A lump formed in her throat, and she attempted another nonchalant shrug. "He told me I'd never amount to much and that I would never find anyone to love me. Stuff like that."

Mateo's jaw was set in a sharp line that could have cut glass. When she dropped her eyes to avoid seeing the fury in his, Mateo didn't appear to like that. He lowered his face closer to hers so she had no other choice but to listen. "He was *wrong*, Nikki. Anyone with eyes can see that you're special. You've got to be one of the most beautiful women I've laid my eyes on."

She couldn't even snort at his comment because he had her so captivated with his words.

He moved closer still until his breath fanned against her face—the heat of it adding to what already hovered beneath the surface of her skin. His focus dipped to her mouth, and his lips parted.

Was he so willing to break the rules just to prove a point? Stealing a kiss was a bad idea, and yet she hadn't wanted anything more in her entire life.

Raucous laughter spilled from the doorway. Mateo immediately stepped back.

Cold air whooshed between them and she exhaled heavily, lashes fluttering wildly. Nikki didn't dare meet his eyes as they stood there in silence.

That had been a close call.

Way too close.

12

———

Mateo

Sophia was dead meat.

Mateo didn't know what his sister had been thinking! Was she trying to sabotage him? Or was she trying to set him up with someone? Because he'd clearly told her he wasn't interested in Annie. Heck, when Sophia had set them up on that first date, he'd only gone along with it because of scenarios like this one. Sophia was incorrigible.

If she was so worried about their family settling down, then she needed to be the one to find someone to fall in love with first. She'd probably seen one too many Keagans fall in love over the past few years.

His jaw ached from all the clenching he'd done since last night. He was on the verge of a mental breakdown with how frustrated he'd become. No matter what he did, Nikki seemed to fill his mind. She took it over and made him want to get closer to her with each passing day.

It wasn't even just her.

The kid was amazing. Each and every one of Paxton's riding lessons had proven just how much the boy deserved to be in a place like this one. If Mateo had his way, he would make sure neither Paxton nor Nikki left the ranch. He'd ensure that Nikki had a job she loved and a place to call her own. And he'd help teach the boy to ride and how to care for the animals.

Mateo caught himself up short. What was he thinking? From the sounds of his own thoughts, it sure appeared as though he wanted something more from Nikki than he'd allowed himself to admit.

"Everything okay, boss?"

He jumped, realizing that he hadn't moved for the last several minutes as he'd let his thoughts send him into a spiral.

Nikki was worth fighting for. That's what this came down to.

He nodded to the wrangler, who adjusted his hold of the ropes he had draped on his shoulder. "I'm fine. Thanks."

The cowboy nodded and headed into the barn behind Mateo. All around them, his men were hard at work. Daniel ran a tight ship, and Mateo couldn't have asked for a better man for the job. Honestly, it should have been harder to merge the business he'd had with the one he dreamed of having.

It was moments like this one when his heart seemed to get cocky. If he could have his dream future with this ranch, then why couldn't he get the girl, too?

It had been difficult, to say the least, opening up about Caroline—and yet, at the same time, it had been excruciating not discussing what she'd done to him. The cathartic result had made that conversation worth it.

And then he'd nearly kissed her.

Mateo groaned, earning himself more than a few strange looks from the men surrounding him. He waved them off and stalked toward the house. He needed to get out of eyesight of these cowboys. The last thing he wanted was for any of the men who worked for him to think he was going crazy.

But as he passed the mess hall he'd built for the people who worked for him, his steps slowed. Last night, he'd brought Nikki home—Sophia, too. His sister's presence had prevented him from talking to Nikki about that near kiss. He would rather choke on his own spit than admit in front of his sister that he was developing feelings for Nikki.

And yet...

He stared at the building, knowing that Nikki was likely inside and getting ready for dinner. He'd avoided her for breakfast and again at lunch. What was the point when, no matter what he did, they were always interrupted?

A sigh burst from his lips, and he continued toward the house. Eventually, he'd figure everything out. Right now, he needed to ignore his growing attraction unless she showed him any indication that she was as interested in him.

A FEW DAYS later and Mateo was cursing his terrible resolve. He stared at the kitchen door from the cafeteria, his brow furrowed. Yesterday, he'd gotten so close to asking Nikki if he could have a private conversation about the night they'd gone dancing. But he'd chickened out just before Daniel materialized, asking Mateo to come check on something.

Now, as he was drilling a hole into the door that separated himself from the woman he felt inexplicably drawn to, he wondered what on earth he was going to say. They still had a professional relationship he needed to uphold.

And at the same time, they had a past friendship that he wanted to believe trumped what was going on now. He'd never been in a situation like this one before. Was he willing to cross that line? Would anyone even care?

Life was short. What if this was the only chance he had at gaining the upper hand of fate? How many times had he told his sister and his friends that he'd ignored fate once and had regretted it every day?

Nikki had been that fate. He'd had feelings for her when he'd been engaged to Caroline, but he'd brushed them aside —buried them so deep that they couldn't be found. And when Caroline had broken his heart, he'd refused to dig them up.

It wouldn't have been an honorable thing to do along that time and he wasn't that kind of guy. But now? Things were different.

He swallowed hard.

Lunch had just ended. She was in there cleaning up. Could he intrude and finally say something?

All he wanted was a chance. That's what he kept telling himself. He wanted a chance to tell her that he liked her, and he wanted to spend more time with her like they had at the club.

Taking a deep breath, he rolled back his shoulders and pushed himself through the swinging door into her domain.

She glanced up at him right away, her smile fading when her eyes met his.

Shoot.

They were alone—which was something he'd been grateful for until she looked at him like he was the last person she wanted to see. This might have very well been a bad idea.

As quickly as she'd frowned, her smile returned. She tilted her head and gave him an inquisitive look. "What can I do for you, Mr. Palmer?"

He bristled at the formality of it all. Ignoring the way it felt to be spoken to like he was nothing more than her superior, he shifted closer and plastered his brightest smile onto his face. Leaning his hip against the stainless-steel countertop, he cocked his head and waited for her to meet his eyes again.

When she did, she stilled—giving him the reaction he'd wanted from the beginning.

"I'll bet you can't guess what I'm thinking."

She'd grabbed a dish from the sink before her and was in the process of drying it when he'd spoken. "No, I don't suppose I can."

"Come on, Nikki. Humor me," he said. "Tell me what you think is on my mind."

The hand holding a dish towel was placed on her popped hip, and she scrutinized him. "What is this about?"

He sighed, moving closer, and he lowered his voice. "I was thinking about how nice it felt when you were in my arms."

It was quiet, but he didn't miss the way she sucked in a breath. Her eyes rounded as she remained pinned beneath his stare. Good. He'd thrown her off balance. Maybe now she'd finally accept that he wasn't just being playful.

Because he wasn't.

He couldn't tear his focus from her. Every flutter of her eyelashes, every sharp intake of air into her lungs—it gave her away.

And he couldn't deny the thrill it gave him to know that he affected her in a similar way that she did him. It gave him the confidence he needed to take the next step—to inquire of her about what he wanted to know most.

"Nikki," he whispered, "haven't you ever wondered what it would have been like if things had been different ten years ago?"

"Sir?"

Inwardly, he groaned. "Don't call me that. Don't call me Mr. Palmer."

"What did you want me to call you?" she said, her voice trembling. They were so near, all he'd have to do was close the inch between them and he'd be able to brush his lips against hers.

"By my name."

She blinked again.

"You think you can do that?"

"Are you sure that's... appropriate?"

"You've called me Mateo before. Why would now be any different? Unless, of course, you're just trying to put distance between us."

Nikki swallowed audibly. "Wouldn't that be for the best?"

"According to whom?" he rasped. "Because I can assure you, it's not in my best interest."

"It's... not?"

Here it was. The moment he'd been waiting for—the

moment where he could tell her exactly how he felt and where he wanted things to go from here. There were worse things than to fall for someone who worked for him—like losing the first chance at love he'd had in over a decade.

He opened his mouth to speak but was cut off by the loud holler of someone entering the cafeteria. "Ms. Reynolds!"

She jumped back from him as her wide eyes flew to the door just before it swung open, revealing a panicked-looking young cowboy. He glanced from Nikki to Mateo and back. "It's Paxton."

Immediately, the room was in an uproar. Nikki charged for the door. "Where is he?"

"He's hurt. He fell from the ladder in the barn."

Nikki was out of the room in a flash of brunette hair. Mateo raced after her, his heart thundering harder than it had when he'd been about to confess his feelings to her.

13

Nikki

ikki's heart slammed into her chest, propelling her forward as she sprinted toward the barn. She couldn't believe she'd allowed this to happen. Paxton had insisted he wasn't going to go anywhere near the barn. He'd wanted to go outside and watch the cowboys work for a while, and she'd figured there was no harm in letting him.

But she should have known better.

Paxton was an inquisitive child. He was also more confident in his own abilities than he should have been at his age.

She didn't even realize tears were streaming down her face until she stopped long enough to look for Paxton the second she'd made it to the barn door.

He sat whimpering, holding his arm close to his chest. He looked up at her, tears drawing streaks down his dusty cheeks.

Nikki gasped, only vaguely aware of the two men behind

her as she rushed for her baby. "What happened?" she demanded, her voice sharper than she'd intended. "You didn't listen to me, did you? I told you not to get into any trouble, and you didn't listen."

"Nikki," Mateo said softly, his hand on her shoulder. "It was an accident."

The mother bear inside her wanted to scream at him to step back and let her handle this, but the woman who was scared to death for her son wanted nothing more than for Mateo to pull her into his arms and reassure her.

These warring thoughts consumed her, made her head spin. It was hard to figure out what this man was beginning to mean to her.

Only when she realized she hadn't said or done anything in response to Mateo did she turn her full focus to her son. Tears still streaked his cheeks, and fear flooded his eyes. "I don't want to move," he whispered. "It hurts."

"What hurts?" Mateo crouched down and reached for the boy's arm. "Here?" He gently squeezed Paxton's wrist and slowly moved up his arm each time Paxton shook his head. When they got to his shoulder, Paxton winced. But then Mateo ran his hand across Paxton's collarbone, and his eyes found Nikki's. "I think he's broken his collarbone. There's a bump right here." Mateo placed his fingers gently to indicate what he'd found.

"His collarbone!" Nikki had to soften her voice and school her features. Her baby broke his bone—because she wasn't supervising him. This was going to come back to bite her. Hospitals were required to report instances like this one. Nikki's heart rate shot through the roof. She fought her instincts to overreact. It wouldn't do any good to get Paxton riled up.

Nikki swallowed hard, her eyes pleading as she met Mateo's. She wasn't strong enough to handle this on her own. Already she felt like she was crumbling.

Mateo, the amazing man that he was, noticed. He turned to Paxton and smiled broadly. "I'm going to take you to urgent care. We'll have someone take a picture of your bones just to have a better idea of what's going on in there. Okay?"

"Will it hurt?" Paxton's lower lip trembled, and Nikki leaned forward to take his hand in hers.

"Pictures don't hurt, kiddo."

"You're mom's right, kid. From what I've heard, broken collarbones are one of the most common breaks."

Nikki gave him a surprised look, but he didn't explain where he'd heard such a thing.

"Do you think you can walk?" Mateo asked. "Are your legs hurt?"

Paxton pointed his toes forward, then up. "No. My legs are okay."

Mateo nodded. "Okay, let's get you to your feet. Careful—don't want you bumping your shoulder on anything." He helped Paxton to his feet, his touch gentle, and it was all Nikki could do to not cry over just how sweet Mateo was being with her son.

During the whole ride to the clinic, Mateo kept the conversation light while getting information out of her son at the same time.

Mateo looked at Paxton through the rearview mirror before tossing a look in Nikki's direction. "Hey, buddy. Did you know that I broke my arm once?"

Paxton didn't respond right away, and Nikki turned to look back at him, finding him staring out the window. She frowned. Had she done more damage than she'd originally thought when she'd gotten upset with him? He shook his head, not giving either of them his focus.

"Well, I did. It was really dumb, too. I was playing tag in the dark with my friends. I tripped on a tree root and landed on my hand wrong." Mateo grimaced. "But the best part was letting people sign my cast."

Paxton swiveled his attention to Mateo. "Do you think I'll have a cast?"

Mateo cut another glance at Nikki. "Actually, I'm not sure. I don't think so."

"Why not?"

He shifted in his seat, and Nikki pulled out her phone to look it up. She offered Mateo a small smile before she answered Paxton's question. "I think they usually just have you wear a sling or something along those lines." She craned her body so she could meet Paxton's gaze. "You doing okay, kiddo?"

Paxton nodded, though his whole demeanor was still sullen. Her chest squeezed. The guilt still racked her body for how she'd reacted to Paxton's fall. She took in a deep shuddering breath as she faced forward and then squeezed her eyes shut to prevent herself from crying right here, right now. She couldn't afford to make him feel worse. He needed her to be strong and calm.

A large, warm hand wrapped around hers. Her eyes flew open to find Mateo staring at her with a mixture of support and concern. He squeezed her hand and gave her a short nod. There was no talking—not with Paxton just a few feet away and able to overhear their conversation.

She nodded back, then mouthed the words, "thank you."

Thankfully, the wait wasn't terrible at the urgent care.

They were able to see the doctor within ten minutes of arrival.

After an exam and a set of X-rays, Mateo's assumptions were confirmed.

"It looks like your son has a break in his clavicle." The young woman smiled with empathy at the trio in the examination room. "I'll put in a referral to see a specialist. They'll be able to tell you how long it will take to heal and what to expect. For now, we'll give you a sling."

"Will I get a cast?" Paxton asked with a small voice.

The doctor shook her head. "No, I don't believe so, not for a broken clavicle. The good news is that the break was clean." She turned to Nikki and Mateo. "That means no surgeries. And for kids, it usually doesn't take as long to heal."

Nikki exhaled with relief. When Mateo took her hand in his, she didn't startle as much as she had before. She gave Paxton a small smile. "Everything is going to be okay."

His lip quivered, and she couldn't take it any longer. Nikki scooped him into her arms as gently as she could. "I'm so glad you're safe." She shifted to place her hands on either side of his face. "I still don't understand why you were on that ladder to begin with."

Paxton looked away. "I wanted to help feed the horses. There was some hay up there that I could give them."

Nikki twisted to look at Mateo. She could get upset with him. To a degree, Paxton's interest in taking care of the horses was his doing. But how could she? Mateo had merely been trying to instill in her child a sense of responsibility. Her son had wanted to help. He'd figured out what he needed and taken charge. To get upset about the situation wouldn't do her or any of them any good.

She swallowed back the frustration and turned her attention back to her son. "Next time, how about you ask one of the cowboys for help—but only after you get permission from me. You weren't supposed to be in that barn. You know that."

He nodded, only briefly lifting his gaze to meet hers. "I know. I'm sorry, Mom."

Mateo moved closer and ruffled his hair. "If you ever want to do something with the horses, you come find me. I'll make sure you stay safe."

Nikki gave him a warning look, and somehow, he immediately understood.

"After you ask your mother, of course," he said with a chuckle.

A shy smile graced Paxton's lips as his focus shifted between the two of them. Today had felt so long, and it wasn't even time for supper.

Mateo brought them back to the ranch and set Paxton up with a movie at the house while Nikki got to work prepping for supper. Her mind continued whirling while she was on her own. There could have been a very different outcome today. She shuddered to think about what would have happened if something worse had happened.

She'd been so deep in thought that she hadn't noticed Mateo's arrival. His presence had a gasp ripping from her throat, and she dropped the carton of green beans she'd pulled from the commercial fridge.

He stood there, leaning against the wall as if he had all the time in the world. Immediately, her thoughts shifted back to what they'd been discussing before her son had gotten hurt.

Chaos erupted in her stomach. She couldn't even think

about anything romantic occurring between them right now. And yet, everything he'd done for her and Paxton was shoved to the forefront of her mind.

Tears prickled behind her eyes, and Mateo's smooth expression shifted to one of concern. He swept across the room without comment and pulled her into his arms. At first, she attempted to push him away, but it had been so long since she'd been wrapped in an embrace like this one. It didn't feel like he was expecting anything from her. Nor did it feel like he was laying any sort of claim on her. It wasn't forced. It was just... nice.

She waited for him to bring up the conversation that had been interrupted—to take her chin in his grasp and claim a kiss from her. While the idea was both thrilling and terrifying, she couldn't deny the relief she felt when he said, "Everything is going to be okay. He's a strong kid. He's already milking his break for all it's worth."

Nikki let out a strangled laugh. "Really?"

Mateo pulled back and swiped at a stray tear with his thumb. "Really. He's got both Sophia and Camilla eating out of the palm of his hand. They made him popcorn and helped him find the perfect movie. When I left, they were discussing the possibility of building a fort."

Her eyes widened. "You're kidding."

His smile did things to her she wasn't proud of, and a sliver of herself wanted that smile to mean more than it did. But this was just the way Mateo was. He hadn't brought up his interest in anything more. Perhaps he'd realized it just wasn't a good time—for either of them.

She refused to be disappointed. She wasn't ready for anything more. She didn't need to be dragged into a relationship with someone as perfect as Mateo Palmer because it would inevitably end in heartbreak.

No one stuck around for her. She'd learned a long time ago that she wasn't meant to have unconditional love. And that was okay. Nikki pulled back and tucked her hair behind her ear with a swipe of her wrist. "Thank you, Mateo. I really appreciate everything you've done today."

He gave her a funny look, and she frowned.

"What?"

Mateo shrugged. "Nothing."

14

Mateo

It wasn't the win Mateo wanted, but it was a win. As he stared up at the ceiling of his bedroom with his hands behind his head, he went over in painstaking detail everything that happened that day.

He'd confessed his feelings to Nikki—well, sort of. And she hadn't run from him or told him he was being highly inappropriate. Before Paxton got hurt, he had the feeling that she might be open to something more.

Then Paxton had broken his collarbone, and Nikki had let him step in and help. He probably should feel guilty over the joy it gave him knowing she was willing to let him take the lead on that. She hadn't pushed him away or asked him to leave them alone to deal with their family matter. And when the nurse mistakenly called him Paxton's father, Nikki hadn't even corrected her.

Of course, that could have been because she didn't hear

it. But Mateo had. And if the small grin Paxton gave him at that very moment was any indication, the kid had heard, too.

Mateo's smile spread wider.

But the best thing that had come from today was that she'd let her guard down enough to call him Mateo again. It probably wouldn't last. She'd call him Mr. Palmer when she wasn't so emotionally drained. That was a given. But until she corrected herself, he wasn't against pretending that he'd gotten one step closer to having something more with this woman.

His chest expanded with a long, slow breath before he blew it out. There was only one problem he could see right now.

Clearly, he was interested, but she was not.

And pushing her to admit feelings she may or may not have would be wrong on so many levels—especially seeing as he was her boss. Shoot! Why did he have to hire her?

He sighed again and rolled over to his side. His feelings had only grown today. He couldn't sleep because he was obsessing over every little battle he'd won. He wanted Nikki more than he wanted anyone in his life—maybe even more than he'd wanted Caroline.

Okay, definitely more.

The man who had loved that wretch of a woman had been blinded by that "first love" haze. He'd been in love with the idea of being with a woman—of having her all for himself. It was a childish, immature sort of desire.

With Nikki, things were different. He could feel it in the marrow of his bones. She was special. She was more than he could have dreamed of having. Part of him had already claimed her as his own, and yet he was nowhere near having her love.

When he'd held her in his arms—to comfort her—he'd gotten a taste. He'd realized what life could be like if she were to give herself over to him and he could be the man she ran to when she needed something or wanted to share in her joy.

His arms felt empty now, and the cravings for more were already getting stronger.

Mateo frowned and forced his eyes to shut. If he didn't get some sleep, he was going to be in a mood tomorrow. It didn't matter if, overall, today was a win. Nikki still didn't belong to him, and something told him he had a long road ahead of him before he got close to getting everything he could have ever wanted.

DANIEL'S CHUCKLE grated against Mateo's nerves. It was low, and no one in the immediate area could hear him. No one but Mateo. "You look like—"

"Don't even say it." He knew he looked like death warmed over. Several restless nights later and he was no closer to getting Nikki on board with something more. He'd said it in his head a thousand times by now—finding different ways to ask her out. And every time he thought he'd figured it out, he second-guessed himself.

He could already tell that Nikki wasn't ready for something—that, or she simply wasn't interested in a romantic relationship with *him*. He'd never admit to how much that idea terrified him. Nikki could be purposefully keeping him at arm's length because of what he'd confessed to her that day Paxton got hurt.

"It's her, isn't it?"

Mateo's head snapped around so fast that he grimaced when pain rattled down his spine. "What?"

Daniel jerked his chin toward the front of the cafeteria area where Nikki brought out a fresh batch of rolls. "She's nice, I'll give you that. And she's one heck of a cook." He turned his smirk on Mateo. "I could see the two of you together, if I'm honest."

Mateo's focus lingered on Nikki for a long while—so long that when she glanced in his direction, she caught him staring. Just as quickly as their eyes locked, they darted away. He couldn't tell from here, but he got the sense she blushed. But that was probably wishful thinking.

Nikki was still keeping her distance. Their conversations had all been too short. The only thing she'd offered him lately was the occasional lingering look and the short, curt conversation.

Paxton, on the other hand, had no such qualms about talking to him. Everywhere Mateo turned, the kid was on his heels, asking about horses and dogs and how big his ranch was or what it was like to be a real cowboy.

Mateo dragged a hand down his face. "It's not her."

"Bull pucky." Daniel snorted. "You forget that I've been around you before she showed up. There's something going on between you two."

Heat swirled in Mateo's stomach—an uncomfortable irritation that stemmed from a combination of frustration over not getting through to her and not sleeping well enough. "If something were going on between the two of us," he muttered through gritted teeth, "you'd see it on her end, too."

His friend chuckled, and they stepped back to get out of the path of one of the wranglers on his way toward the food.

Daniel had his arms folded, but his stance was relaxed. It wouldn't take much effort at all to tackle him to the ground and demand he stop making comments about Nikki. It wasn't the talking about Nikki that was the problem. It was the teasing, the jesting that the two of them actually had a chance—when Mateo couldn't see past the wall she'd built around herself based on the sole fact he was her employer.

Daniel stared at him with one brow arched, the smirk fading somewhat. "What's the problem? If you like her, do something about it. You have to make a decision at some point. Either she's worth the chaos, or she's not."

She was definitely worth it.

Nikki was worth the biggest storm, the hardest of winds; she was worth more than Mateo would ever vocally admit to Daniel. But the risks continued to hold him back. In a way, he'd been shut down by Caroline, and he wasn't sure his heart would be able to handle getting broken again.

That was the point of Daniel's comment, though, wasn't it? Was Nikki worth the possibility of getting his heart broken? There was only one answer that came to his mind.

And he knew exactly what it meant.

Nikki's eyes found his, and she gave him a small smile. That smile was all it took for Mateo to make his decision. The next moment he could get her alone, he'd finish the conversation they'd started a few days ago. One way or another, she'd have to make her own decision.

Mateo nodded, offering his friend a tight smile. "You're right. I can't keep sitting on the sidelines."

Daniel's surprised gaze followed Mateo as he left the building. He didn't call after him, thank goodness. Mateo wasn't sure he could handle the conversation continuing at this point. The last thing he wanted was to lose his nerve.

MATEO STRODE toward Nikki's door, passing those of his siblings down the hallway, and then he skidded to a stop. Clenching and flexing his fists, he stared hard at the door like doing so would allow him to see through it. Everyone had turned in about an hour ago, Nikki included. From what he could hear, Paxton wasn't up and moving around. There was a light on that he could see beneath her door.

Nikki was still up.

He took a step toward the door again, then stopped himself and brought his fist to his teeth. Hadn't he told Daniel he was going to do something about his attraction? He couldn't be the coward that he'd been since she'd shown up. It was now or never.

Forcing himself to move another step onward, he lifted his fist and rapped his knuckles quietly on the door, then held his breath. If she didn't answer in the next few seconds, he would slip away and pretend he hadn't come at all.

As if his feet jumped on board with that idea before he was ready, they shuffled backward. But the knob turned, and he forgot to breathe altogether.

Nikki opened the door, and her eyes met his. "Mateo?" she whispered. "What are you doing here?"

He bounced his fist against his thigh and shrugged. "I live here."

She smirked, glancing behind her shoulder. She slipped from her bedroom and came out into the hall while closing the door behind her. "What did you need?" Her voice was still low, and her brows were pulled together with concern. "Is everything okay?"

"Yeah," he breathed. "Everything is fine." He let his focus

sweep over her, from the way her soft waves of warm chocolate hair framed her face to her toes that peeked out from beneath her bright red and pink pajama pants.

Nikki fidgeted expectantly.

He cleared his throat and nodded. "Right. I wanted to talk to you."

"Okay..." she drawled.

Once again, he coughed to clear the lump that refused to stop blocking his airways. He brought his hand to his back and rubbed it as he dropped his gaze. "I wanted to finish that conversation we'd started when Paxton broke his collarbone." He met her eyes just as they widened, but he couldn't tell if it was from fear or something else entirely.

"Mateo—"

"Before you say anything, hear me out. I want to take you on a date—a real one. Just you and me."

"Why?" she blurted.

"Why?" he repeated. "What do you mean, why?"

She shook her head, her cheeks flushing a deep pink color.

Mateo didn't wait for her to answer his question before he answered hers. "Because I think you're beautiful."

Nikki scoffed, and he frowned at her reaction.

"I'm crazy about you," he said, stepping closer to her.

She flinched, holding her hand up. "No, you're not."

He let out a surprised laugh. "Because you're so in tune with *my* feelings? What do you mean?"

Nikki dragged her eyes from his and scooted back so she leaned against the bedroom door. "You just... it's nothing."

"No, you can't say something like that and brush me off. There's no way for you to know what's in my heart unless I tell you. And right now, I'm telling you that I want you." He reached for her hand and held onto it firmly despite the gasp that escaped her.

Part of him wanted to tell her that he'd had a crush on her all those years ago and this felt like a second chance, but he didn't think she'd believe him. It felt like she'd push him away. Or maybe she'd resent him for not acting on that crush when they'd been friends. Either way, telling Nikki anything about his past feelings wasn't going to happen.

He took a deep breath and blew it out through pursed lips. "Don't push me away, Nikki. I've already been having one heck of a time trying to ignore the attraction I've developed for you."

"You have?"

Was he mistaken? Or did she sound almost hopeful? Mateo took a risk, reaching out with his free hand to trace a line down her jaw. "I have."

She shut her eyes at his touch, and he stifled a grin. He was getting past her defenses.

"Let me prove it to you."

Her eyes flew open, and she stared at him with those bright eyes.

"Let me take you out and show you how I feel," Mateo pleaded. He waited, holding his breath as she considered his offer. Suddenly, she nodded.

"Okay," she said. "One date."

"That's all I need," he promised, bringing her hand to his lips before brushing a kiss across her knuckles.

15

———

Nikki

Nikki lost count of how many times she'd pinched herself. She was actually going on a date with *the* Mateo Palmer. This was either going to blow up in her face or be the best night of her life. She glanced at Mateo out of the corner of her eye as she sat in the passenger seat of his truck for the second time within a week.

He hadn't told her where they were going. She figured they'd be getting dinner and then doing something more. Honestly, she wasn't going to be picky. As long as she was going to spend time with Mateo, she was going to be happy.

Every few minutes, he glanced at her. It was like they'd gone back in time and the two of them were in high school again. The tension hung so thick in the air that it was difficult to breathe right. Something needed to give so they could just get back to being comfortable in each other's company.

Nikki wrung her hands in her lap, trying to come up with

the words to apologize for acting so weird, but there was no way to say it without making her sound like a simpering fool. They were not teenagers. He wasn't the popular jock, and she wasn't the shy wallflower. They were adults who had grown up and were very capable of chasing after something more with whomever they wanted.

Somehow, Mateo found her hand and slipped his fingers between hers. He squeezed tight and flashed her a smile that had her legs going weak and her heart fluttering wildly. If they didn't get more than just this night together, she'd be grateful for the chance.

Tonight, she'd make a promise to herself. There would be no chasing after something that wasn't meant to be, so she'd simply enjoy his company.

Nikki glanced out her window just as the country club came into view. Her eyes cut to Mateo with confusion. "Why are we here again?"

One side of his mouth lifted into a grin. "The last time we were here, I didn't get nearly enough time with you in my arms. I fully intend on monopolizing all your time and holding you every last second."

Her first instinct was to laugh him off. But his eyes and his voice were so serious that she couldn't bring herself to utter a single sound. Not a single degree of mirth or teasing was evident.

Was it possible that he'd been telling the truth this whole time?

Nikki swallowed hard and smiled right back. "Well, if you're game, then I am."

She didn't think it was possible, but her words had his smile widening further. It made the swirling, twirling emotions within her go into overdrive.

It was fine. This was totally fine. Eventually, the thrill of this night would fade away and she'd get back to feeling normal again. Until that time, she'd give in and enjoy the evening. She reached for the door handle, but Mateo's sharp voice startled her enough that she yanked her hand from it.

"No."

She turned wide eyes toward him. "Why? Are we going somewhere else first?"

He shook his head. "You're my date, and as such, you'll be treated like it. I'm opening that door for you, so don't you even think about getting it for yourself."

Nikki rolled her eyes with a smirk but did as she was told. She watched him walk around the truck to her door. He pulled it open and held out his hand for her to take. She eyed his offering and placed her hand into his before he helped pull her to her feet and into his arms.

She gasped as his face came within inches of hers. For a second, she expected him to steal a kiss, but his lips came within millimeters of her ear. His breath grazed the sensitive skin there when he whispered, "If our date ended right now, it would still be the best one I've ever had."

"Why's that?" she rasped.

"Because you said yes." He withdrew from her, his eyes blazing with the honesty of his words.

"You really shouldn't say stuff like that to me," she said under her breath.

"Why not?" he ground out, surprising her with the ferocity that laced his words.

Nikki gaped at him.

His expression softened as he reached out to caress her face again. "I'm going to tell you something right now, and I expect you to believe me and drop whatever this hesitancy thing is you've got." He didn't wait long enough for her to retort. "I asked you out because I wanted to spend time with you. I get that this might seem strange because of our past, but it doesn't change the fact that this is where we ended up. So, we're going to go into that building, eat until we can't take another bite, then dance the night away."

Nothing sounded better than what he'd just described. And she berated herself for allowing those doubts to once again creep into her mind. Mateo wasn't her ex. He was nothing like any of the men she'd spent time with.

She took in a deep breath and nodded.

After they enjoyed a steak dinner, Mateo didn't waste any time taking her through the building toward the dance floor. There were no pretenses, no dancing around the fact that he wanted her close.

Immediately, his arm reached around her back, and he pulled her so tightly against him that she had no chance of escape. His eyes poured over her features before returning to her eyes. She couldn't think of a single time when he hadn't been smiling while they were together.

It wasn't lost on her that they'd gotten their share of looks. This town might not be tiny, but it was small enough for people to know who Mateo was. She wouldn't have been surprised to find out that he'd dated every single woman who gave her the side-eye.

But Mateo didn't seem to notice. He only had eyes for her, and it thrilled her to no end.

They swayed and danced to the music, allowing her to abandon any notion that Mateo wasn't being anything but honest. With each passing song, she started to believe it herself.

When they were both out of breath and needing some

fresh air, they exited the building and took a walk out on the balcony. Mateo held her hand, his thumb tracing over the back of it as they found a place away from prying eyes.

She leaned up against the building, letting her gaze roam up his body to his face that hovered inches from her own. He moved in closer, resting his forearm against the brick above her as he stared right back at her.

"You're beautiful, you know that?"

A smile tugged at her lips, and she looked away, but she couldn't resist his gaze and looked at him once again.

"I mean it. I don't know if you've been told enough because clearly you don't agree with that sentiment."

Her mouth fell open, and a slice of indignation raced through her. "I don't think I'm ugly," she snapped without thinking. "I'm very happy with the body that God has sought fit to bless me with."

His smile only widened, which spurred her to continue.

"But I'm also not an idiot. I know what society deems beautiful and what you—" She snapped her mouth shut and her eyes widened as the full weight of what she'd nearly admitted came crashing down on her.

He arched a brow, his lips turning down slightly. "What I... what, Nikki?"

She shook her head and attempted to move out from beneath his stare, but he boxed her in.

"No, none of that," he said, his voice drilling deeper into her soul with each syllable. "You keep saying stuff like that, and I want you to tell me exactly what you think it is I'm feeling."

Nikki pressed her lips together. He wasn't going to let her go without an explanation, but this wasn't supposed to be the moment she told him that he'd been shallow his whole life so he couldn't possibly find her attractive.

Heat burned beneath her flesh, and in a moment of desperation, she reached up with both hands and framed his face between them.

Mateo stiffened only briefly at her touch, but then he allowed her to pull him closer. Her lips claimed his, tasting his sweet essence and tender affection. He slipped an arm around her waist to pull her even closer to him. The arm that had been above her head had lowered as well, and he placed his hand behind her neck.

This kiss was nothing like the ones she'd experienced before in her lifetime. It was passionate and all-consuming. It spoke of a desire that neither one of them seemed capable of sating. She melted into him, giving her entire soul to this kiss and wishing for it to never end. The way Mateo reacted to her touch said it all.

He wanted this as much as she did. And she'd been silly to assume he was anything like the men in society who refused to date women with real curves.

Their kiss ended the second someone exited the building and moved in their direction. Nikki was breathing harder than before, her heart stumbling over itself as she found Mateo's piercing gaze.

He had a bit of a smug told-you-so look on his face, but she found she didn't care. As far as she was concerned, they'd both won something tonight.

She stifled a laugh and fell back against the brick as she dragged a hand through her hair. But in the next second, he dipped his face closer to hers once more. His lips grazed hers, just a whisper of a kiss before he trailed his touch along her jaw and toward her ear.

"You're something else," he said against it.

Nikki shivered, the chills rippling through her body in the most pleasurable way possible. She let out a shaky breath as he pulled back and stared down at her like she was a treasure worth hiding away from the whole world. Placing a hand to his cheek, she let out a sigh. "And you're everything I never expected."

They stared at one another for what felt like an eternity. Finally, he wove his fingers in between hers and jerked his chin toward the dance room. "What do you say we get in a few more songs before we head home? I'm not ready to give you up just yet."

She tightened her hold on him and nodded. "I'm all yours."

Mateo brought her hand to his lips for what felt like the millionth time that night, and yet it still made her stomach churn with anticipation of what all of this meant. Then he winked at her. "Promise?"

His question gave her pause, but only for a moment. "Promise," she whispered.

16

———

Mateo

ateo nodded to the barista in thanks as he grabbed the cardboard cup carrier. Two coffees and a hot chocolate. For the most part, the coffee shop was dead. People didn't come to town to get an early coffee fix—at least not in Copper Creek. Those who got their usual tended to be those running errands or going to their jobs in the hub of town.

His brothers and sisters had still been sleeping when he'd left this morning. The guys who worked for him wouldn't be getting their breakfast for another half hour. But he'd heard Nikki get up a little less than an hour ago. She'd slipped down the stairs and headed out to the building where she fixed everyone's meals.

It had been hard for him to sleep after the night they'd had. Mateo was stuck on the high he'd gotten from simply being in her company. If his experiences last night taught him anything, it was that he wanted more—needed more. Walking away from Nikki at this point would be a mistake. It would be walking away from fate.

And he wasn't going to do that.

Not again.

He arrived at the ranch with fifteen minutes to spare. Granted, there was a chance that the men would start to drag themselves from their beds and head for breakfast early, but they didn't go into the back.

Except the two who helped Nikki with meals occasionally.

Mateo wasn't worried about them. They'd likely have figured out that something was brewing between Nikki and himself. So far, they didn't seem concerned with it.

He whistled to himself as he headed up the couple of steps to the breakfast hall. With sure, quick steps, he made his way past the rows of tables and toward the kitchen door. Just as he'd thought, the two cowboys were helping Nikki finish up with meal prep. All three of them looked up when he entered.

Nikki's eyes flickered with something.

Desire?

Adoration?

Surprise?

It didn't matter as long as she wasn't scowling at him.

He jerked his head toward the door. "I'd like a minute with Ms. Reynolds."

The two cowboys exchanged quick glances with Nikki, who only smiled reassuringly at them. Mateo moved closer to her, waiting until the men were through the door before he spoke. He kept his voice low, so if the cowboys were eavesdropping, they wouldn't be able to hear what he had to say.

"I had a really good time last night," he said, plucking the coffee he'd bought just for her from the cardboard carrier.

Nikki's eyes dipped to the drink and a smile curled her lips. "Me too."

"Good."

She lifted her focus to him and tilted her head with amusement. "Good?"

He nodded. "Good."

"Why's that?" she crooned.

"Because I want to do it again."

She huffed a soft laugh. "I don't know how often I can get away to go dancing—"

"Not dancing."

"Oh?"

Mateo shook his head slowly and pointed to the smaller of the three cups. "You know what this is?"

She glanced at it, then shook her head. "Should I?"

He chuckled. "I got Paxton a hot chocolate."

That seemed to surprise her. Nikki's mouth dropped open slightly as she exhaled. "Why would you do that?"

"Because I like him." He leaned closer still. "And I like you." When she remained silent, he had to chuckle again. "Nikki, I *really* like you. I thought it would be nice if we spent more time together, and I know that means spending time with Paxton."

She blinked several times. "You... want to spend time with my son?"

He reached forward and traced a line down her jaw, smiling when she shivered at his touch. "Let me take you and Paxton for a ride. He's been getting real good at riding."

"That was before he broke his collarbone." She shook

her head. "It's not a good idea for him to do any physical activity—"

"I'll make sure he's not jostled. He can ride with me on my horse. I swear he'll stay safe. We can go for a short ride to this great place we have on the eastern side of the property. We can make an afternoon of it—take a picnic. We can bring music and play some games. It'll be great."

She bit down on her lower lip as she considered his offer. Already, he could see that her hesitation was fading. All he had to do was tip the scales in his favor and he'd get what he wanted.

"We don't have to go today, of course. But we could do it on Saturday. That will give you a few days to prepare something simple for meals so you won't have to worry about feeding the men."

"He would probably like to get out of the house," she lamented. "He's been going stir-crazy since he broke his collarbone. And since he can't do his riding lessons until it's healed..."

"Exactly. This will be perfect for him."

Nikki stared at him, her focus diving deeper into his mind and his soul. He shifted beneath that scrutiny, wondering if he'd pushed too much too soon. Technically, they'd only been on the one date. Nikki didn't seem like the type to want to jump into something so quickly.

He placed the cardboard cup carrier on the counter at his side and took her hand in his. "I don't want to rush anything if you're not comfortable." Even as he said the words, his heart lurched. There was a part of him that was worried if he didn't hold tight to what he'd found with her last night, he'd lose it.

For a moment, she didn't move. But then she shook her

head. "I don't feel like you're rushing anything," she hedged. "And Paxton is clearly comfortable with you. I don't see why we couldn't do something on Saturday. You're sure it would be okay for him to ride with you?"

He expelled a breath of relief. "Positive."

"Look, Mom! Look, there's a bird over there."

Mateo's arm tightened around Paxton's waist. "Easy, kid, you're squirming too much. Can't have you falling off this horse or your mother will have my hide."

Paxton twisted his head around to grin at Mateo. "Sorry," he said.

A chuckle reverberated from Mateo's chest. Up until he'd gotten to know Paxton, he hadn't realized just how fun it was to spend time with a kid. When he'd dated Caroline, he'd known he'd wanted children. He'd planned on having a big family just like his parents. Unfortunately, that dream had died along with his marriage.

Now, it was coming back to him, and it didn't terrify him nearly as much as he'd thought it would.

His eyes glanced to Nikki's from where she rode her own horse. Man, he loved seeing her smile. She had to be the most beautiful woman in the world, and he got the strongest feeling that she'd never quite see that.

It wouldn't matter how much he told her; she'd always see herself as less than others that surrounded her.

Nikki's eyes all but sparkled as they continued their ride. They'd passed a fox, numerous pheasants, and other birds in the trees. Paxton had missed the rabbit that skittered across the trail because he'd been distracted by a different critter.

Each and every animal that captured the kid's attention had him twisting and squirming in the saddle. Mateo had long since gotten used to his movements, but that didn't mean his heart didn't stutter with each jerky motion. He'd sworn Nikki's kid would be safe. He wasn't going to let her down.

Nor would he let down this little boy.

They made it to the picnic area. Nikki dismounted first so she could get Paxton from the saddle and his feet on solid ground. Mateo followed suit.

"Okay, kiddo. I have a big favor to ask of you. It's really important. Do you think you can help me out?" Mateo said.

Almost immediately, Paxton straightened his shoulders and puffed out his chest. Between that stance and the cowboy gear he wore, he definitely looked like he belonged here. And that fact made Mateo's heart swell. Paxton grinned and nodded. "Okay, good. I'm gonna need you to find the best place to put our picnic blanket. Do you know how to pick a good spot?"

Paxton nodded resolutely. It took everything in Mateo's power not to react to just how awesome this kid was.

Mateo held out the blanket to the boy. "Can you carry it under your good arm? Or do I need to help?"

"I can do it," he said firmly.

Mateo could feel Nikki's eyes on him throughout the whole exchange, and she only approached him when Paxton hurried off with the blanket in hand.

She sidled up beside him and slipped her hand into his. "You're really good with him."

He cut her a look out of the corner of his eye. "He's a good kid. Makes it easy."

Nikki leaned into him, and the tightness in his chest

increased. He couldn't remember the last time a woman made him feel this way—like he belonged solely because he wanted to be claimed by her. Spending time with her had been amazing. It had fueled his desires in a way that hadn't happened in years. But being here with her boy?

It completed him in a way he hadn't realized he needed.

Mateo pulled his hand free and wrapped his arm around her shoulders, pulling her close and kissing her temple. He could get used to this—being here with her, with Paxton—having them be a part of his family.

"Thank you," she whispered just as Paxton called out to them.

"Here!"

Mateo glanced down at her. "For what?"

She turned her eyes up to meet his. "For including him. For making him feel special."

"He is special." As much as he wanted to kiss her, to claim her lips for his own selfish needs, Paxton called out again.

"I can't get the blanket spread out. Can you help me?"

Nikki's lips parted with a soft laugh and a smile. "You're being summoned."

"I can't think of a better reason to leave your side."

She laughed again with a roll of her eyes as she shoved him in the direction of her son.

He walked backward, his palms up. "You're going to owe me, though. Next chance I get, I'm stealing that kiss."

Nikki's blush said it all. She was enjoying this as much or more than he was. Nothing could get more perfect than the moments he spent with her. Fate was finally smiling down on him—giving him everything he'd ever wanted and more.

If he stayed on this trajectory, in a few months he could see himself asking for her hand.

Of course, he wouldn't be telling her that. Nikki needed more time. He could sense it. But as for his heart, he knew exactly what he wanted, and it was to be part of her family.

Mateo winked at her. "How about you make yourself useful and get our supplies? I'm sure Paxton is completely famished after his hunt for the perfect spot."

Nikki was practically glowing. He hadn't seen her this happy in all the time he'd known her.

And he'd been the one to make that happen.

17

———

Nikki

It had been a month of Mateo outwardly showing her affection.

Thirty days of attention from the man she'd secretly had a crush on in her formative years.

And no sign of him changing his mind—no sign of him losing interest.

As much as Nikki had been waiting for Mateo to prove he was like most of the men in her life, she had to admit he wasn't showing any signs of heading in that direction. He wasn't as shallow as she'd thought. Even though he'd dated women who could have been models in another life, he genuinely seemed to care for her despite her not being anything like those women.

It had gotten to the point that Nikki couldn't deny that Mateo was even more perfect than she'd built him up to be in her mind.

And the way he was with Paxton?

She could have thrown herself at Mateo and begged him to be hers forever just for that alone.

Every time she turned around, she found her son watching Mateo with awe and a smidge of determination. Nikki could see just how much Paxton looked up to this man —this cowboy who had become a sort of superhero all on his own—and she suspected he didn't even know.

Her eyes locked with his across the small expanse of property as he sat beside Paxton on a bale of hay. They were working on knot tying, which was more than a little difficult seeing as Paxton still struggled with his arm to his chest. The good news was that his bone had healed rather quickly. Apparently, children's bones could do that better than those of an adult. Nikki couldn't be more grateful.

Mateo smiled at her, and a rush of heat rippled through her body. He wasn't outwardly affectionate with her more than their quiet moments of chatting, but there had been more than one occasion where she'd met him in the kitchen after Paxton had gone to bed. And she couldn't forget the way he'd pulled her into the kitchen when no one was there so he could steal a kiss.

When he smiled at her like that, all she could think about was how good it felt to be wrapped in his arms.

There was just one thing holding her back, and she wasn't proud of it.

Mateo still wouldn't confide in her about Caroline beyond what he'd said at the Country Club. He didn't want to hear about her or talk to Nikki about anything related to her. Nikki couldn't help but wonder if he still harbored feelings for Caroline. Was there a chance he was suppressing those feelings for Nikki's benefit? For him to hold onto that pain for so long had to mean something.

The thought made Nikki's stomach twist uncomfortably. She could imagine all her organs bunching together and cowering from the part of her that knew they needed to air out those memories. It would be smart, right? Mateo should be capable of telling Nikki he was past the pain and heartache.

And if he wasn't?

She pushed down the negative thoughts as she tore her eyes from the man she had grown to love more than she wanted to admit. She hadn't told him—mostly because she was terrified. She didn't want to jinx what they had that was going so well.

The more she thought about Caroline, the more the woman haunted her. Nikki hadn't heard from the woman in so long, and yet she still infiltrated her thoughts and made it difficult for Nikki to truly enjoy what she had.

She could already imagine what Caroline would do if she heard about Nikki's budding relationship with her ex. She'd make a scene. Even though they weren't friends anymore, Caroline would pull the "sisters before misters" pact they'd made in high school.

A sigh built up in Nikki's chest. She wasn't going to go there. Thinking about Caroline would only poison her heart, and she'd left that part of her life behind her. If Mateo wanted to keep Caroline out of their lives, who was she to argue?

"Hey," a soft, deep voice murmured behind her ear. She gasped as two arms wrapped around her waist.

Nikki's first thought was to look around them to make sure no one was watching, but apparently, Mateo had no such concerns. He pulled her back against his chest, and his warm breath sent goosebumps pebbling across her skin.

"Is everything okay?"

She pulled at his hands, breathless. "Mateo, you... what are we..." Her voice was lost when she felt him nibbling at the skin of her neck. "We... is this smart?" she whispered. "Anyone could see—Paxton—"

"I'm tired of hiding what I feel for you," he responded without hesitation. "We've been dancing around this relationship of ours, and I'm certain everyone knows anyway. No one has lodged any complaints. We might as well make it official."

"What does that mean?" Her breath hitched in her chest as her grip on his arms relaxed and she allowed herself to lean into him. Whatever it was, she was ready. He was right. While sneaking around had its merits, she was more than willing to move on to the next phase of their relationship.

"My family is having a game night tonight."

She stilled, attempting to turn in his arms, but his hold on her tightened. "Okay," she drawled. "Is there a reason you're telling me this?"

He chuckled, sending a fresh wave of chills erupting down her spine. Just the sound of him was enough to affect her, but combine it with his touch? And her legs felt like a goopy mess. If he wasn't holding her, she might have literally melted into a puddle on the ground.

"Mateo," she whispered in warning when his teeth grazed against the shell of her ear.

"I want you to come," he said. "You and Paxton."

"But it's a *family* game night."

"And one day you, might be part of it."

He couldn't be saying what she thought he was saying.

She didn't want to allow herself to believe it. This was all happening so fast. It was too soon, right? And yet she'd known him for so long. She'd just only recently stolen his affection.

Would she really be rushing things if she allowed herself to give in to this man who had swept her off her feet and allowed her to believe in love again?

This time when she turned in his arms, he welcomed it.

"Come with me to game night. I'm pretty certain that my siblings know what's going on between us, but I want to make it official."

He wanted to lay claim on her publicly. That had to mean something. She smiled, unable to help herself as she lifted her palm to his cheeks. Before she could utter a word, Paxton's voice broke through the quiet.

"Are you guys going to kiss?"

Mateo grimaced comically, and she turned to find her son with a wrinkled nose and his head tilted with curiosity. He didn't look upset, so at least they had that going for them. It was more of a concern if anything. Her heart twisted in her chest, and she hoped that wasn't an indication that he'd been aware of everything that she'd gone through when it came to the men in her life.

"Yeah," Mateo announced, to which Nikki gasped. "Because I like your mom a lot. Is that okay with you?"

She whacked him with her fingertips and shifted to move away from him, but his hold remained firm yet again. Her eyes shifted to her son and she waited, holding her breath to hear his answer.

Paxton took in a deep breath and let it out his nose as if he had to concentrate hard on what he was thinking about. Then he heaved a sigh. "I guess."

Well, that wasn't a "no," but it didn't feel like Paxton was completely on board with this situation, and she couldn't figure out why. He adored Mateo. Wouldn't he be thrilled about the idea of them being together?

Before she had much of a chance to think about what was coming next, Mateo grasped her face in both of his hands and promptly kissed her forehead.

Relief and disappointment burned through her, followed by amusement as Paxton laughed at Mateo's antics. She smiled at her son, then lifted her adoring gaze to the man who knew how to read the room.

They did learn one thing, though. Paxton's feelings about their relationship would need to be worked through. She needed to figure out what was bothering him so they could tackle it head-on.

Mateo released her and turned his attention to Paxton. "We're having game night in the living room tonight. You want to join?"

Paxton's focus shifted to his mother with question. "Can we, Mom?"

"Of course, sweetie. I think it sounds like it would be a lot of fun."

Her son grinned wider. "Yeah. It does."

Nikki could feel every single pair of eyes on her as she sat beside Mateo on the couch. Her hand was in his as he spoke.

"Since we have guests, we should ask them what they want to play tonight." He squeezed her hand, then gave Paxton a wink. "What do you say, kid? What are we playing tonight?"

Paxton glanced around the room, eyes wide as he took in Mateo's family. It wasn't that he was nervous. Nikki knew that expression. This was something else. Awe perhaps? She didn't have any siblings, and neither had Dennis. Whenever they spent time as a family, it was just the three of them. And here her son sat among seven adults who were giving him their undivided attention. He rubbed his nose with the back of his hand, then glanced at her. "Can we play Pictionary?"

At least two of Mateo's siblings groaned. Three of them grinned.

Mateo chuckled. "Absolutely."

They spent a good couple of hours playing the game. Mateo picked Paxton to be on his team every single time. Nikki could see her son coming out of his shell more and the admiration Paxton had for Mateo returning.

Every so often, Mateo would catch her attention and wink at her, making all kinds of fluttering feelings explode in her chest. No matter how much she tried to squash them down and remind herself that just because times were good right now didn't mean they always would be. Things could change in an instant. All she could do was enjoy the time she had with this amazing man and not plan too far into the future—if only to keep her heart safe.

By the end of the night, Paxton and Mateo were in the lead. Sophia and Nikki worked together, and Nikki got the feeling Sophia wanted to say something but kept whatever it was to herself. The other siblings pulled in lower scores and eventually called it quits.

"Rematch," Camilla and Isabella insisted as one.

Mateo smirked, pulling Paxton to his side with an arm around his shoulders. "I'm sure we can wipe the floor with you again. This kid is a whiz at drawing."

Paxton had a beautiful glow about him as he stared up at Mateo, and Nikki's heart constricted. He'd never looked at Dennis that way. Then again, Dennis hadn't been all that interested in being a father. He'd been kind—but that was where his affection ended. He hadn't wanted to adopt her son. He hadn't wanted to raise him.

Nikki's eyes shifted to Mateo, wondering just how involved he would be if they were to do as he'd suggested earlier and start a family.

Something told her things would be very different than they'd been with Dennis, and she couldn't say she'd ever be disappointed by that.

He caught her eye and smiled. She returned it with one of her own. Yes, she could definitely see a future with him. And he'd make a wonderful father, too.

18

———

Mateo

That's weird.

Mateo stared at his phone at the unknown number. He never got text messages from people other than his contacts. Granted, he'd gotten a handful over the years from people who had the wrong number, but this one was addressed to him.

UNKNOWN: *Mateo, I want to see you.*

HIS THUMB HOVERED over the option to delete the message. He didn't know why he hesitated. If he didn't have the number saved in his phone, he didn't need to know who it was. The fact that they knew his name had to be the only reason.

And yet his gut was telling him he should just ignore it and move on. If it was important enough, they could call. Or they could tell him who they were.

He stared at the message and then shook his head before closing out the app and shoving the phone into his pocket. Whoever it was could reveal their identity if they wanted information from him.

Allowing himself to brush off the strange feeling he'd gotten from the message, he thought back to a few nights ago when he'd finally mustered up the courage to have Nikki included in his family activities.

He'd noticed the strange behavior from some of them. They knew of Nikki's relationship with his ex. And for all he knew, they were only wondering if Mateo had lost his ever-loving mind.

Maybe he had.

How else did one describe when they fell in love after having their heart broken?

He couldn't help it, though.

Nikki was like the spring rain after the harshest of winters. She was the first sign of green sprouting and the first kiss of warmth from the sun. He could already feel himself releasing the reins he'd clutched so tightly for so long.

And she was everything.

So was Paxton, for that matter.

When the time was right, he'd make sure they both knew he had every intention of claiming them both. He didn't know the full extent of Paxton's parentage, but he would do whatever it took to become that boy's father.

His phone buzzed and he frowned again, pulling it out of his pocket.

Then his heart dropped out of his chest and landed with a thud at his feet.

Unknown: *I can tell you saw my message. If you want to ignore me, turn off the read receipts. It's been almost ten years. I would have thought you were over what happened.*

There was no denying who this person was. He'd deleted Caroline's information and blocked her for good measure when they'd broken up. Apparently, she had a new number but hadn't lost his.

Mateo glowered at the message, tempted to ream her out and tell her to go where the sun didn't shine. He wanted to tell her everything he hadn't had the strength to say back when she'd ripped his heart into ribbons. He wanted to let the festering anguish rise up and burn with the fury of everything she'd done to hurt him.

The irony of his situation wasn't lost on him. Nikki still tried to bring up Caroline. Sometimes outright, sometimes she'd ease into it.

Every single time, he'd shut her down. When he'd brought her up that one time, it had been the last. He'd promised himself as much. It was like Caroline had become a demon of some kind. Nikki had said her name too many times and now she was showing up.

Well, Mateo wasn't going to let her steal his happiness a second time. He wasn't going to allow her to slink into his life and claw apart the pieces he'd finally put back together after she'd cheated on him and moved on with another guy.

Why was she reaching out now? There wasn't a good

reason for it. She had no excuses. Like she'd said herself. It had been about ten years. What kind of monster waited for ten years to reconcile with the person they betrayed?

What makes you think she's trying to reconcile?

The question was like a slap to the face.

She wanted to meet, and there would be no telling why unless he responded.

Heat filled his whole body, and he shook his head with disgust. He couldn't believe he'd actually considered responding to her for a moment there.

He tapped his phone until he'd blocked the number and deleted it. He didn't live under a rock. If she'd figured out her last number had been blocked, she'd figure out that this one had, too. Eventually, she'd message him again. And he'd do the same thing with that number until she got the hint.

For the rest of the day as he went through his usual work with the dogs and check-in with Daniel, Mateo kept going back to those messages he'd gotten from Caroline. Part of him knew it would be better just to hit this head-on. She wasn't going to stop. He'd known Caroline well enough to figure that out.

She'd try with the messages, then phone calls, and then she'd probably track him down through social media. If she got that far, she'd likely get his address. His business was common knowledge. She'd figure out where he lived...

His whole body froze, hand on the gate of the corral he was just about to enter as he realized what that would mean. If Caroline showed up here, she'd realize that Nikki was here. There was no telling how that scenario would play out. She could lash out at Nikki... or her son.

Caroline was a terrible person, but she wouldn't hurt a child, would she?

Mateo shrugged away from those thoughts and forced himself to think about better things. Caroline's message had put him in a tailspin, and he needed to right himself before he saw Nikki later today. She'd be able to tell if something was wrong, and he was definitely not going to tell her that Caroline was trying to reach out.

Nothing would spell trouble like that news coming to the forefront of everyone's notice.

He shoved himself into the corral and shut the gate behind him. Daniel and two of his other wranglers were getting some new horses ready for a trial run with the cattle and some of their freshly trained dogs. If everything went smoothly, the dogs would be sent off to their new families and the horses would be given a permanent home.

If not, they'd be working with the dogs some more and the horses would be evaluated as to whether they stayed or were auctioned off. Mateo didn't have time for stubborn beasts, no matter how tender Sophia's heart had become toward the animals.

"Ready?" Mateo ground out.

Daniel's eyebrows rose as his head swiveled to look at him. Mateo grimaced inwardly at his sharp tone. Already, he was letting Caroline influence his work. This wasn't good. If he couldn't contain his fury around his friend, how on earth was he to do so around Nikki?

"Sorry," Mateo muttered, gripping the saddle horn to launch himself into his seat. "It's been a long day."

"It's not even lunch yet," Daniel mused.

"Don't remind me," Mateo said, his eyes shifting to the building where Nikki worked. "You know the plan? We're going to move the cattle to a new pasture that's farther out and see how the dogs do. Then, in a few days, we'll bring the cattle back."

Daniel nodded curtly. "The guys know what they're supposed to do. And we're all set."

Mateo stared down at the three dogs they were taking on this trip. Each one sat, waiting for them to get going. Roman beamed with pride. With how busy Mateo had been with Paxton's riding lessons and spending time with Nikki, he'd delegated more responsibility to his brother in training the dogs. He wouldn't be coming on this ride with them, but he'd brought the pups to the corral so Mateo didn't have to track them down.

Offering his younger brother a nod and a smile, he jerked his chin toward the mess hall. "I'm going to be gone most of the day. Will you keep an eye on the kid for me? He's got a knack for slipping away when his mother is busy. I really don't want him breaking another bone now that the sling will be coming off next week."

Roman nodded. "Sure. I'll distract him with something. Or maybe I'll get Sophia—"

Mateo set him with a warning look. "Sophia is working with the horses today. We need to keep the kid away from the larger animals until we know he's healed completely."

Roman rolled his eyes. "You've become such a buzzkill. You know that?"

Grinning, Mateo couldn't deny the joy he felt in knowing why his brother had that opinion of him. Mateo was settling down with a beautiful woman and her son. He was taking responsibility in a way he'd never done before. If that meant he was getting boring, he couldn't think of a better reason.

The ride was uneventful. The dogs did their jobs with little to no mistakes. Even the horses seemed to be on their best behavior. It made Mateo wish it had been more difficult because then his mind couldn't wander. He hated himself for allowing his thoughts to consistently drift to that woman.

By the time they returned, he was mentally spent. He didn't want to face Nikki for fear she'd notice and demand that he open up to her. He had to be stronger than this. She deserved a better person who didn't immediately get tugged back into a storm where he had no right being.

Mateo dismounted his horse and offered to brush down the others, sending Daniel and his other men to dinner. He took his time, focusing on clearing his head from everything related to Caroline.

Then his phone buzzed, and all his dismal thoughts came roaring back to the surface. He gritted his teeth and pulled out his phone. Thankfully, it was a message from his sister wondering if he was going to eat dinner with them or if she needed to save him a plate so Roman didn't eat everything.

He sent off a quick reply and pushed out a deep breath.

"Everything okay?"

Nikki's soft voice had him flinching far more than it should have. She was behind him. How long had she been there? Shoot! Had she noticed his reaction to his phone?

Slowly, he turned to face her, noticing the lines drawn between her brows. He smiled and nodded. "I'm okay. It's just been... a day."

Even he could see that she didn't believe him. It was clearly written on her face. He'd gotten to know the little nuances of her expressions. When she was worried, it wasn't easy to rid her of those emotions. And right now, the woman he cared about was concerned for him.

Nikki reached toward him, and he welcomed her into his

arms. She held onto him, resting her cheek against his shoulder and breathing deeply. "I'm sorry."

Those two words normally would give him a bit of peace. But all he felt right now was guilt. He should be confiding in her. He should be telling her what he was dealing with, and yet he was being a coward.

No.

He was being stubborn.

Caroline didn't deserve to infiltrate the joy he'd found with Nikki, so he would protect what he had at all costs. No matter what it took, he'd keep Nikki shielded from the woman who had influenced their lives for the worst.

Nikki pulled back to look at him, the concern still etched into her face. She did smile, though. And it appeared that she wasn't going to push him on what he was dealing with.

"I'm the luckiest man alive," he said, brushing his lips to her forehead. "Because I have you."

19

———————

Nikki

"Now we get to celebrate!" Nikki whooped. "No more wearing your sling." She nudged Paxton with a laugh. "What do you want to do?"

Her son grinned up at her, though he held his arm to his side with a noticeable amount of caution. "Do you think Mateo will let me start my riding lessons again?"

Nikki ruffled her son's hair. "It wouldn't hurt to ask." Though, deep down, she wasn't sure how Mateo was doing. Lately, he'd been distracted. It wasn't that he was distancing himself from her. There wasn't a single day that they didn't spend some time together. She'd gotten to know him on a much deeper level than she had when they were younger.

There was just a niggling feeling of discontent that refused to disengage from her mind. Mateo was struggling. And he wasn't willing to open up to her.

"What's wrong, Mom?"

Nikki startled and glanced down at her son. It was then that she realized that she'd been frowning. Hmm. She needed to get better at hiding her concerns from her son. He was already too intuitive for his own good. He had a knack for seeing when she was down. Forcing a smile, she reached for him and tickled him until his own worry lines disappeared from around his brows.

"How about you and I get some ice cream on our way home from the doctor?"

"Can we get something for Mateo?"

"Sure, buddy. What do you think he'd like?"

Paxton made a show of considering the question and what his answer should be. He tapped his chin and stared up at the sky before holding up his finger. "I know. We should get him a giant cookie."

She laughed. "Yeah? What kind. The bakery has sugar cookies, chocolate chip cookies, snickerdoodles—"

"Definitely chocolate chip," Paxton said with finality. "He likes chocolate chip cookies like me."

Nikki couldn't contain her additional laughter. If there was any proof that Paxton had begun to accept the relationship she had with Mateo, it was how close the two had continued to become. There were only a few short-lived moments when he didn't seem sure about them. It usually only occurred when Mateo completely blocked out the world and it was just him and her.

She could understand Paxton's concern when that happened. He'd experienced being overlooked when she'd been dating Dennis. She'd expected their relationship to improve over time, but Dennis simply didn't connect with her son. The tipping point had been when Dennis told her firmly that he had zero interest in adopting Paxton—right in front of her boy.

They'd gotten divorced shortly after that.

Nikki pulled open the car door for her son and gestured for him to climb inside. She gave him a reassuring smile before shutting the door. Mateo had never said one way or the other if he'd want to adopt Paxton. She liked to think that if she asked him to, he'd be on board with her request.

A thrill coursed through her, and she couldn't wait for that point in their relationship to come to pass. She slid into the driver's seat and glanced through the rearview mirror at her son. He was looking out the window, a happy expression on his face.

They picked up their desserts and made their way back to the ranch. The second they arrived, Paxton took off in search of Mateo.

"Careful, bud!" she called after him. "I don't want you getting hurt again." But he was too far away from her to hear her. That kid was fast when he wanted to be. She shook her head with a chuckle as she dipped back into her car and retrieved her phone. It lit up at that moment with a notification from her social media app.

She frowned.

CAROLINE HARRIS HAS SENT *you a message.*

HER HEART LEAPED into her throat, and she glanced up as if reading Caroline's name was all it took for the woman to materialize. Nikki had blocked her friend after their falling out about five years ago. From the looks of it, Caroline had made a new profile.

Nikki swallowed hard as she stared at that message while her stomach clenched. They hadn't left things on good terms. Whatever this message was, it would surely be related to how things had ended, and Nikki didn't want to deal with such a confrontation. She grimaced as she considered the two choices before her.

She could respond, or she could ignore her. It wouldn't hurt to see what Caroline had messaged her, though, right? Nikki would be able to get a good feel for what Caroline wanted. And what if she'd finally seen the light? What if Caroline wanted to reconcile?

Nikki had been raised to be kind to others even if they'd wronged her. She could give Caroline forgiveness. And if Caroline was just going to be her regular old self? Well, then Nikki would ignore her and not bother messaging her back.

She nodded as if the movement alone was all she needed to give herself strength to follow through. Then she opened the message from her ex-best friend.

Hi Nicole! It's been forever. Can you believe how long it's been since we hung out? I heard from Heather that you moved out of Colorado Springs and to some tiny town. I always thought you were more of a small-town girl. I bet it suits you so much better. Guess what! This is hilarious. I'm going to be visiting Copper Creek next week and we should meet up! I can't believe that fate has put us in each other's lives again! And if everything goes well, then maybe we can keep hanging out. Missed you, girl!

·   ·   ·

NIKKI GAPED as she read the message a second time. No apologies. No mention that they'd gotten in a fight. It was like Caroline didn't remember anything about what happened between them. She actually wanted to meet up. It was ridiculous.

Or was it?

She started second-guessing her own memories of the two of them. Nikki had been upset with Caroline, but maybe she hadn't made it clear enough. And if she never told Caroline that she'd been hurt, Caroline wouldn't know.

But she had to know. Not even Caroline was that dense.

Nikki huffed a sharp breath and shoved her phone into her purse. She wasn't going to dignify Caroline's message with a response. She refused to admit even to herself that she was irritated with not only Caroline but herself for allowing the woman to worm her way back into her mind after everything was going so well.

It didn't matter that Caroline had once been engaged to Mateo.

Nor did it matter that Mateo avoided any conversation about the woman.

Right here, right now, he belonged to Nikki. And she belonged to him.

At that moment, the source of her affection came sauntering toward her with Paxton at his side. He'd already taken a bite out of his cookie, and Paxton couldn't be more thrilled about it.

Nikki's heart surged like it did every single time she saw them together—her adorable little family. She couldn't tell Mateo that, though. Not yet. She needed to make sure Mateo was all in. He needed to be fully healed from his shattered past, and she wasn't sure he was just yet.

Mateo didn't waste any time closing the distance between them. He claimed her lips with a searing kiss that left her breathless.

"What was that for?" she breathed.

"That's a thank you."

"It is?"

He lifted the cookie. "For this."

Nikki chuckled and glanced down to see a flicker of a frown on Paxton's face before he grinned.

"See, Mom? I told you he'd like it."

"You sure did, kiddo," she agreed. "I'll make sure I never question you again."

Mateo ruffled Paxton's hair. "Paxton was telling me all about how his collarbone is healed up and is as strong as ever. Looks like we're going to resume our riding lessons."

Nikki fought the urge to tense. After Paxton got hurt, she was nervous, to say the least. But as long as her son was willing, she wasn't going to stand in his way. The look on her face must have said it all because Mateo turned to Paxton. "We're not gonna be able to go riding today, but Sophia made some fresh lemonade. I bet if you ask real nice, she'll get us some to drink while we relax on the porch before dinner."

Paxton frowned, his impatience shining through. Surprisingly, he didn't argue. He took another bite of his ice cream and turned to rush for the house. As soon as Paxton was out of earshot, Mateo leaned in close and tucked a strand of hair behind her ear. "Don't worry. I'll make sure he stays safe."

"You can't guarantee that," she said, her eyes following Paxton as he ran. "But it's something I've grown accustomed to."

He frowned, his touch tracing along her jawline. "You're upset about something."

Nikki blinked. Geez! Why was she so transparent? She needed to guard her emotions better. Mateo shouldn't be able to tell from a single glance that she was struggling with something. "I'm fine," she blurted.

Mateo arched a brow. "Is this about Paxton riding? Or is it something else?"

It was a culmination of things. Yes, she was worried about Paxton. And she was concerned about Mateo holding back from her. Then there was the message from Caroline. Nikki sighed. "Just thinking."

"Good thinking? Or bad thinking?"

She wanted to laugh, to cover up her weaknesses. But he was being so totally sweet she couldn't avoid what she said next. "Being a mom means being prepared for the unknown. The future isn't promised, and all that. In a second, something can happen to change fate."

"That sounds really dismal," he said, his voice sad and contemplative.

"Not really," she said, tilting her head and gifting him with what she prayed was a warm and reassuring smile. "We have to hold on tight to all of the good in our lives, enjoy it, and be grateful for each and every moment." She lifted her hands to his face and framed it between them. "You're one of my happy moments."

"I'm not going anywhere," he rasped, and his words filled her with a scorching heat that ripped through her body, blasting all her doubts into dust. That was what it was like, being here with him like this. There was good and bad in every relationship. Eventually, he'd confide in her. *Eventu-*

ally, he'd trust her enough to open up and give her everything.

Life was too short to waste it on wondering and fretting.

She pressed a gentle kiss to his lips. "I know," she whispered.

Her thoughts shifted to Caroline's message. Life was too short to hold onto the pain of the past, too. If Caroline didn't think there was anything wrong between them and was reaching out to rekindle something...

Well, Nikki didn't have to become her friend, but she didn't have to completely ghost her either. She could meet with Caroline and tell her that she'd moved on from their friendship. It didn't cost her anything to be kind.

While that idea didn't cause her inherent joy, it didn't seem nearly as bad as she'd originally thought. Nikki was the better person, and she wasn't going to let anyone—let alone Caroline—drag her down.

Mateo grabbed her hand. "Come on. Let's get that lemonade. And you can show me those X-rays that Paxton is so excited about."

She laughed. "Sounds like a plan."

20

———————

Mateo

"Did you find what you were looking for?" The florist standing behind the counter smiled brightly at Mateo, her eyes warm and sparkling. There was a lilt to her voice, one he was incredibly familiar with—one that he'd used frequently when winning women over.

That time of his life was over.

There was only one woman for him.

He nodded, pulling out his wallet to purchase the bouquet he'd picked out for the love of his life. "This is all I need."

"Would you like me to write anything on the card?"

He considered it for a moment. "For the girl from my past, and the one I want in my future."

The florist crooned as she nodded and wrote what he'd dictated. "That's so sweet."

"Thanks," he said.

The last week had been strained. He wanted Nikki to know just how much she meant to him, no matter how tough things got.

Caroline had been persistent. She'd managed to track him down on social media and commented on several of his business posts for the ranch from different accounts. She'd private-messaged him and told him that she was going to be in town soon and wanted to meet up. He'd ignored every message. He had no interest in seeing her or speaking to her.

That woman was someone he wanted to keep in his past. She would have no part of his life or what he'd created from the ashes of her betrayal.

The florist handed him his card back along with the flowers. "I'm sure she'll love them."

He smiled. "Yes, she will. Thanks."

Mateo stepped out of the floral shop, a whistle on his lips and a skip in his steps. He couldn't wait to see the look on Nikki's face when she saw the flowers he'd bought for her. He'd never gotten her flowers before, but he couldn't imagine that she was one of those girls who would prefer something else.

Who didn't love flowers?

Even if she didn't like them, he'd figure out what she did like, and next time he'd make sure to get it for her.

He'd spend the rest of his life making sure she knew she was loved just like she deserved. No one deserved to be cherished more than Nikki. And no one deserved to feel as though they belonged than her amazing kid.

A woman collided with him just outside of the bookstore, and she gasped as the flowers nearly fell from his hands. "I'm so sorr—" Another gasp tore from her lips, followed by a sharp giggle. "Mateo? Oh my gosh, Mateo! I can't believe we actually bumped into each other!" Caroline squealed her delight, her hands reaching out and grasping his forearms with both of her hands. She even jumped a little.

It was all overkill and reminded him so much of why he disliked her.

Mateo gritted his teeth until his jaw ached. He gripped the flowers dangerously hard as well. Seeing her brought back flashes of memories he had long since buried. And along with them came the debilitating pain.

All he could think about was how desperate he'd felt when he saw Caroline's mother walk down the aisle with that look on her face.

Pity.

Apology.

He hadn't realized why Caroline had abandoned him— not until a few hours later when word got to him that she'd left with one of her brother's friends. They'd run off into the sunset with each other, not caring that Mateo was left behind to pick up all the shattered pieces of his wedding. It had destroyed him to the point that he couldn't bring himself to speak of it after that day.

She squeezed his arms, and he tore away from her.

"There's a reason I didn't respond to your messages, Caroline. I don't have anything to say to you."

She pouted like she hadn't ripped his heart from his chest and stomped on it. Then she flipped her hair and placed a hand on her hip. "I know I hurt you, Mateo."

He scoffed, but that was all he could muster.

Caroline frowned, her expression dissolving into something that resembled guilt—or as close as someone like Caroline could get to it. "I wanted to clear the air."

"I don't need the air cleared. I've moved on. And I'm sure you have too."

"That's just it," Caroline said, inching closer to him. "You don't know how much I've agonized over what happened between us."

Mateo hated how much that confession brought him satisfaction. This wasn't him. This person who was callous and unforgiving. And yet, she was the woman who had turned his world upside down and left him in pieces.

She reached out to touch his face, but he jerked away from her. "Don't." His voice wasn't as strong as it should have been. It was as if he'd used up all his energy simply reliving his past, that he couldn't fight her off if he tried. He swallowed down the lump in his throat. "Don't touch me."

Caroline had the good grace to nod and look somewhat chagrined. "Will you get coffee with me? I know it's a lot to ask, but I..." Her voice trailed off, and emotion filled it unlike anything he'd heard from her before.

It tugged at his heart in a way that made him feel sick inside. He shoved down that feeling and straightened, waiting for her to continue her plea.

"Please let me try to make this right."

There was no making this right. They both knew it. So why was he still standing here, considering it?

Because Nikki would want him to get closure. She would want him to heal. And what better way to do that than to let Caroline say her piece. He didn't have to agree to anything more.

"Fine," he ground out.

Her eyes widened with excitement and relief. "Thank you."

He nodded down the street. "There's a shop just down here."

"I was actually on my way over there." She looped her arm through his, and he pulled back from her.

Mateo wanted to tell her not to touch him again, but he had a feeling it would fall on deaf ears. And he wasn't going to waste his breath trying. So instead, he took a few measured steps away from her.

When they got to the coffee shop, he pulled the door open for her and followed her inside.

The coffee shop wasn't terribly busy—a fact that unnerved him. No one in Copper Creek knew who Caroline was. Hardly anyone had heard about the embarrassment that was his failed relationship. In fact, as far as he knew, no one had heard the story. And that was how it would stay.

Still, the gossip mill had already gotten wind of the bachelor from Winding Creek Ranch and the girl from his past that had stolen his heart. He and Nikki had received more than their fair share of glances from the older women in town. They were all smiles and gushing congratulations. It was strange and mildly embarrassing, but nothing more than he'd expected.

If any one of those women caught him with Caroline at this coffee shop, he'd have a lot to explain about if Nikki caught wind.

He grimaced at that thought alone. There was a good chance that Nikki wouldn't understand. And he wasn't going to risk it.

So, he avoided ordering himself a coffee and chose

instead to move to the table in the corner of the room—far away from the windows facing the street.

Caroline was seated soon enough. As she pulled out the chair across from him, she smiled like she'd won something. His stomach knotted. He didn't want her winning anything —not after what she'd put him through.

Taking a deep breath, he reminded himself this would be the only time he allowed a meeting like this one.

Caroline wasted no time in batting her eyelashes and treating him like she always had. She reached across the table and traced a fingertip along the back of his hand. "How have you been?"

He scoffed. "I thought you wanted to clear the air."

She frowned slightly, then nodded as she retreated. "I've been working on myself, Mateo. I want to be better. And out of everything I've done in my life, you are my biggest mistake."

Mateo could believe that.

Caroline made a move to touch him again, so he dropped his hands in his lap, the bouquet of flowers resting on the table between them. Her eyes snagged on them as if seeing them for the first time. For a long moment, she stared at them before she lifted her gaze to him. "Those aren't for one of your sisters, are they?"

He shook his head, tempted to tell her that he'd fallen for her best friend—the very woman who Caroline had thought was beneath her. But Mateo knew he wouldn't take pleasure in Caroline's pain. He was over that part of his grieving. And he didn't want to bring unwanted attention to Nikki in case Caroline ended up reaching out to her.

"Is it serious?" she asked.

"Yes."

"Who is she?"

"Does it matter?" he said. "We're not here to talk about my girlfriend. We're here to hash out what happened between us so we can both move on. I take it that's what you wanted to do when you sought me out. That's usually what people do when they're trying to make something more of themselves."

She flushed, the first sign that she might be telling the truth. She cleared her throat and placed both of her hands in her lap. "You're right." She dropped her gaze to her hands and fiddled with them before she said, "Does she make you happy?"

"She does." The warmth returned to his voice, causing her to look up at him. "And for what it's worth, I hope you're happy too."

Caroline smiled at him, but he needed to shut down the hope she had shining in her eyes.

"That being said, I don't want you to contact me again."

It took all of a few seconds for fury to blaze in her gaze. The coloring in her cheeks deepened, and her jaw tightened. "But—"

"No buts. I don't owe you anything else. And you don't owe me anything."

"How dare you," she seethed.

He stiffened, his own anger returning. He'd given her a chance to apologize, but all she seemed interested in doing was turning the conversation over to him. What did she think this would be? Did she actually believe that he'd take her back with open arms? Because that was what this felt like.

"You seriously want me to believe that you've found someone better than me? I mean, I know that I hurt you, but you clearly weren't over me. Otherwise, you would have been married by now. I bet you anything that you barely know this woman, whoever she is. And soon enough, you're going to kick her to the curb because she won't compare to me."

He leaped to his feet, his hands slamming on the table with enough force to have it shuddering. "You're right. She's nothing like you. She's a hundred times better than you because she would never hurt the person who loves her the way you hurt me."

Emotion flickered in Caroline's eyes. Anger, surprise, pain, then triumph. "See? You love me."

"I *loved* you," Mateo emphasized. "I really did. But the second you walked out on me with someone else, that love fizzled out. I don't love you anymore. And there's nothing you can do to change that." He stormed for the door without waiting for her to respond. She'd manipulated an emotional response out of him, and he hated her for it.

It had been a mistake to meet with her. He should have told her to leave the second he'd bumped into her.

Mateo got all the way to his car before he realized he'd left the flowers behind. A groan dragged itself from his lips, and he rested his forehead against the steering wheel. There was no way he'd go back for them. He couldn't risk seeing her again. And that meant he wasn't going back to the floral shop either.

Caroline was smart. If she really wanted to corner him, she'd figure out a way to do that. And those flowers were ammunition.

21

─────────

Nikki

Nikki couldn't breathe. Her brain had ceased to communicate with her lungs as it was wholly distracted by what she was staring at. Rubbing her eyes wouldn't help, no matter how much she wished it could. Her worst fears had come to fruition, and now she was left a hollow shell of herself, not knowing what to do.

She spun from the sight of Mateo and Caroline sitting at a table in the coffee shop where she was supposed to be meeting Caroline in about five minutes. There was no way this wasn't planned. Caroline must have somehow figured out that Nikki was involved with Mateo. This was Caroline's way of showing just how superior she was.

Chatter, car engines, and other sounds felt like they were coming from somewhere far away. Her ears weren't picking up the subtle nuances of the city with all the blood rushing in her head. Heat crawled and seared beneath her skin as she slinked away from the door in desperate search for somewhere to hide. She couldn't be caught staring. That was what they wanted. And yet she couldn't just bail, either.

Caroline was a conniving woman who knew how to get what she wanted, and she wanted Nikki's pain.

Squeezing her eyes shut, Nikki gulped in breath after breath as she leaned against the building in an alleyway. She'd wait for Mateo to leave. She'd have her coffee with Caroline. And then...

Then, *what*?

It wasn't like she had anywhere to go. This job at the ranch had been the best option for her. It provided her with a place to stay, food, and even childcare for the most part. There was nowhere else she could have possibly gone to get the deal she had now.

The heat in her face intensified as she considered what would happen if she stayed. She'd have to see Mateo every day. She might even have to witness him with Caroline again. Dread filled her. She couldn't believe he'd go back to her.

Maybe he hadn't.

That desperate thought wriggled its way into her heart and took root.

Maybe she'd walked in on something that he had a perfectly reasonable explanation for. That was possible, right?

Nikki wanted to cry. No, she wanted to scream. She wanted to march right back to that coffee shop and confront the two of them—demanding answers.

Okay, no, she didn't.

A groan burst from her lips, and that sick feeling in her stomach returned. She didn't have the courage to confront the two of them—at least not together. She didn't think she'd be able to stand seeing the look of guilt on Mateo's face as he told her he was sorry but he was still in love with his ex-fiancée.

Nikki covered her face with her hands and focused on her breathing, not caring that people wandered past the alley and gave her strange looks. She'd go into that shop as planned. She'd tell Caroline to crawl back into the hole that she'd clawed herself out of. Then she'd tell Caroline that she'd lost.

Her hands dropped to her sides, and she turned toward the entrance of the alley. Slowly, she crept to the edge, her eyes sweeping along the street in search of Mateo. There was no sign of him. Hesitantly, she emerged from the alleyway and strode toward the coffee shop, stopping at the edge of the large windows that let in all the natural light the shop could ever need.

Immediately, her focus landed on Caroline. She was alone.

Thank goodness.

Her lungs filled slowly, and she exhaled as she moved with purpose to the door and pulled it open. She ignored the line for coffee, her stomach swirling too much to allow her any sort of food or drink, and she marched right up to the woman who had only ever done more damage than good.

Caroline's eyes darted upward as soon as Nikki's shadow crossed over the table. Her eyes brightened, and her perfectly painted, red lips curled into a grin that Nikki knew all too well.

Nikki opened her mouth to let her have it, but Caroline cut her off.

"Did you know that Mateo lives here?" Caroline didn't

wait for an answer. "It's insane. I never thought he'd be the kind of guy to settle so far from his folks. He'd always talked about working on a ranch... but *owning* one?" Her voice was tainted with a sort of desire—no, coveting—that only made Nikki's stomach turn more. "He's done really well for himself." Caroline's shrewd gaze flitted up to Nikki. "Well? Are you going to sit down? You're hurting my neck making me stare up at you like that."

Fingernails bit into Nikki's hands, a deep-seated sense of protectiveness pulsing through her body. Caroline didn't want Mateo back because he was the one who got away. She wanted him back because he had some other value to her. "You've seen him?" Nikki said, her voice holding an edge that apparently Caroline didn't hear.

She nodded, her smile widening even more. "Today, actually. We got coffee. And he gave me these." She reached for the bouquet of flowers at her side and brought them to her nose, inhaling deeply. "They're beautiful, aren't they?"

Nikki stared at the flowers skeptically. "He did?"

For once, Caroline looked offended. "You don't think he would get me flowers?"

Oh, how Nikki wanted to wring this woman's neck. Instead, she feigned nonchalance and shrugged. "You did leave him at the altar."

Caroline's eyes narrowed venomously for a moment, and then she flashed a wide smile. "There's something to be said about irresistibility. You see, some guys know what they want, and even if their heart is ripped from their chest, they'll keep going back to it. I'm that something for Mateo."

Nikki scoffed. She'd see about that. The second she had a chance, she'd ask Mateo what he thought of Caroline.

But hadn't she already tried bringing up his ex before?

He'd brushed her off so many times she'd lost count. Did that mean something? Was he hiding how broken up he still was over her?

Caroline's sharp gaze cut through Nikki's defenses as she let out a bark of laughter. "What is that sound for? Do you think you'd have a chance with him?"

Nikki avoided Caroline's gaze. Once upon a time, she'd thought she had a shot. But looking at those flowers, she wasn't so sure anymore.

The wretch of a woman must have noticed her attention on the flowers because she waved them in front of Nikki's face. "You don't believe that he'd get me flowers, do you?" She plucked the card from the little plastic holder that had been shoved among the arrangement and flicked it in Nikki's direction. "All you have to do is read that to know I'm telling you the truth."

The card had landed front side down. Nikki itched to flip it over and read what he wrote to Caroline, but she was too terrified to reach for it.

Caroline groaned, her patience worn thin as she reached forward and turned the card over. "See? It's there in black and white. For the girl from my past, and the one I want in my future." It was undeniable. And the worst part was that he'd signed his name at the bottom. "That's me. Who else could it be?" Caroline sniped.

She made an excellent point. Mateo hadn't dated anyone else in high school. Nikki couldn't recall anyone else who would fit the note.

"I'm gonna win him back. Because who wouldn't want someone like me?"

At that, Nikki eyed the woman who used to be her friend. Caroline was still beautiful. She might have had some work done—Botox, maybe. She was still slender or toned, and she was nothing like Nikki. If she was who Mateo wanted, there was no way Nikki would stand a chance. That knowledge deflated any ounce of fight she had left.

"I see you haven't really taken care of yourself." Caroline's words snapped Nikki from her despair. Her eyes swept over Nikki with a curl to her lip. "Maybe if you did, you would be married by now."

"I was married," Nikki muttered.

A huff of laughter escaped from Caroline. "But you're not anymore?"

"We got a divorce. What about you? Doesn't seem like the guy you chose over Mateo is in your life anymore."

Caroline flipped her hand dismissively. "Yeah, well, I left *him*. A long time ago, actually. She returned her focus to Nikki with curiosity. "You dating anyone? Or is the divorce still weighing on you?" She pouted out her lower lip as if she really cared, but Nikki knew better. She was fishing for more information—more she could hold over Nikki.

"I am dating someone, actually." Just the thought of Mateo, though, struck her in the chest with an ache that wouldn't ease. Nikki rubbed at the spot above her heart, but that didn't help matters at all.

"Well, if you're not careful, it could end the same way your divorce did. Maybe you should go to the gym more. Cut some calories." She gave her a pointed look. "Guys like it when you take care of yourself, you know. They might humor you in the beginning, but if they can tell that you're not going to change, they're on to the next person."

"Is that how you felt about Mateo?"

Caroline cast such a dark look in Nikki's direction that it might have burned her if she had been any closer. "Mateo didn't want to change. He was content to let life pass him by. He didn't have dreams or plans for his future besides working with his folks on a ranch with other guys who didn't graduate from college." She shrugged. "So I left. And guess what? It worked. Mateo picked himself up by his bootstraps and made something of himself."

Nikki hated how Caroline could rationalize what she'd done to Mateo. She'd cheated on him, for heaven's sake. This wasn't just a matter of her leaving. "Have you ever considered that Mateo might have gone and made something of himself with you by his side?"

She seemed to think on Nikki's words a bit, tapping her finger on her lip before she shrugged. "I guess we'll never know." Caroline shifted her attention to the flowers and allowed her fingertips to graze the petals of a carnation. Then her eyes lit up, and she turned to Nikki. "I'm going to be here for at least a week. We should catch up while I'm here. You know, pick up where we left off."

Nothing sounded worse than spending more unnecessary time with this woman. She was like an illness that Nikki couldn't seem to cut from her life. She opened her mouth to say as much, but the phone on the table to Caroline's right flashed and buzzed.

Caroline didn't even hesitate before picking up the phone and turning it over to see who was calling. Any normal friend would have declined the call, sent it to voicemail, or asked if it was okay to answer it while out with someone else.

But not Caroline.

She simply answered the call and held up a finger to Nikki.

"Sarah! Hey! It's been forever. How are you doing?"

Based on that answer alone, Nikki knew the call would drag on. She knew Caroline had all but dismissed her. The longer she sat in front of Caroline, the more she hated that she'd allowed herself to get wrapped up in a friendship with her in the first place.

Caroline was no friend of hers.

Nikki sighed, slipping out of the chair where she sat. "Goodbye, Caroline."

Her friend waved a hand at her. "Oh my gosh, I know, right? Who would have ever predicted that?"

Nikki didn't look back as she slipped from the coffee shop and headed for her car. Well, that meeting couldn't have gone more wrong if she'd planned for it.

22

Mateo lifted the fist of wildflowers he'd gathered for Nikki. He had a vase for them. While they weren't as flashy as the flowers from the shop, they suited her better anyway. They were wild and unique, not cultivated the way society thought they should be. He probably should have gotten them to begin with.

A smile tugged at his lips despite the sour way his afternoon had turned out. Caroline might have tracked him down and pushed her way into getting coffee with him, but she wasn't going to take away the happiness he'd found with Nikki. He'd kept that part of his life secret from Caroline, and he couldn't have been happier about that.

He marched into the house with his handful of wildflowers and hunted for the vase he knew was around somewhere. His sisters had gotten vases throughout the years from the occasional guy. They wouldn't mind if he borrowed one.

The flowers looked good on the kitchen table. He stared at the vase with a tilted head, wondering if he should have at least picked up a card. Notes were nice, but saying something in person would probably be better.

Yes, something in person would be better for sure. Nikki seemed like the type who would prefer something thoughtful straight from the source.

He headed to his office to get some paperwork done. Nikki's car hadn't been out front, so she was likely running errands. Paxton wasn't running around outside, so either he was with his mother, or he'd found some cowboys to spend time with. Or maybe one of Mateo's sisters was watching him.

It was nice having the kid hanging around. He felt like one of the family already, and Mateo was looking forward to the day when he could make that permanent. The warmth that spread through his chest at the thought of officially forming a family with Nikki and her son had him reeling. Not even a few months ago, he'd never thought of himself as a family man in the traditional sense. A forever bachelor? Sure. But a dad?

He chuckled to himself, his thoughts going haywire rather than staying focused on his work. Maybe it was time he spoke to Nikki about all of this. She should know where he stood when it came to her boy. He couldn't imagine she'd be upset.

Mateo lost track of time as he struggled to remain focused on the task at hand. There were documents he had to file, invoices he had to send out, and records he needed to send to his accountant, for heaven's sake.

The door to the front house opened and then slammed shut as quick footsteps darted through the house and toward the stairs. Paxton had been living here long enough to be able to recognize his steps. Mateo pulled back from his desk and stood, intending to see who was with the boy when he heard her exasperated voice.

"What did I say, Paxton? No running."

He frowned. She didn't sound happy. More like she sounded exhausted. Mateo moved farther from his office and caught sight of her as she started up the stairs. Their eyes locked. She didn't smile at him. Her expression was tight as her focus darted upstairs, then back to him. "Hey," he said.

"Hey," she said with a sigh.

That didn't sound good. He should get her the flowers. He should pull her into his arms and tell her that whatever was bothering her would turn out okay. He had to do something, right? His fingers twitched at his side, and he nearly took a step toward her but stopped himself. "Everything okay?"

She glanced again up the stairs. Was something wrong with Paxton? He didn't sound upset. Nikki's shoulders slumped, and she came down the stairs before lingering at the base. "Can I ask you something?"

Mateo moved toward her. "Of course. You can ask me anything."

She gnawed on her lower lip, and he got the feeling she wanted to look anywhere else but at him. Something was definitely wrong. He could feel it in the way the hair on the back of his neck stood on end. What happened today to send her into this mood?

"Nikki," he said, reaching a hand out to her. When she

gave a short shake of her head and wrapped her arms around herself, he dropped his hand to his side. The disappointment slithered inside him like a venomous snake, ready to strike.

Everything was okay. He was getting riled up over nothing. Just because she was having a bad day didn't mean it had anything to do with them. She would have told him, right? Nikki didn't play games. It was one of the things he liked about her. She was upfront about everything.

She heaved a sigh and finally lifted her gaze to meet his. "What were you up to today?"

Was that all? She wanted to know about his day? He blew out a nervous breath and chuckled. "I ran some errands in town. Had to drop off a few things at the post office. Picked up some feed from the store." He wasn't going to talk about the flowers or his visit with Caroline. There was no use in sharing that part of his day. Mateo rubbed the back of his neck, offering her a boyish grin. "I picked you some flowers."

There was a flicker of interest in her eyes as she stared at him, but it quickly died down into smoldering embers of what might have been. "That's it? That's all that you did?"

He almost felt like she wanted him to say something more. But that was ridiculous, right? She didn't know about his visit with Caroline, and if he had his way, she never would. Mateo shrugged. "That's it. Nothing to write home about. You wanna see the flowers?"

She huffed, shaking her head as she muttered something that sounded almost like, "I should have known better."

"What?" he asked, moving close enough to grab her hand, but she side-stepped him, refusing to let him touch her. "Nikki, what's wrong?"

Her scowl knocked him off balance. "Nothing," she

snapped. "It's been a long day. I'm exhausted. I have to go fix dinner soon, and Paxton wanted to go for a walk. I have to go."

"I can go with you—"

"No," she snapped, his head whipping backward at her tone. "No," she tried, softer this time. "I told him it could just be him and me. Mother-son time, you know?"

He tried to ignore the pain of rejection. They were still their own little family, no matter how much time he'd been spending with them. Occasionally, they were going to want their own time. Still, Mateo couldn't shake the feeling that something had gone terribly wrong today and he needed to do something to help.

Letting her go right now wasn't something he was prepared to do. This time, he reached for her and captured both of her hands in his own. "Hey," he said softly, waiting for her to lift her gaze to meet his. When she finally gave him what he sought, he pushed through the ache and focused on what he could do to help. "You know I'm here for you, right?"

She blinked rapidly and a flush crept across her skin, her eyes filling with emotion. But she looked away before he had a chance to get a full grasp on her reaction to his words. "Thank you, Mateo." Her words were barely above a whisper. "But I'm fine. I don't need you to rescue me or do anything for me right now. I've had a bad day, and I just want to spend some time with my son."

He opened his mouth to argue, but Paxton's voice drifted toward them from the upper level.

"Mom? Are you ready?"

Mateo's eyes landed on the boy, who was now dressed in his boots, hat, and pair of jeans. He looked like he belonged on the ranch. Heck, he looked just like Mateo had when he was a kid. Mateo grinned at the boy, and Paxton grinned back.

"Are you coming, too?"

Before Mateo could accept the invite, Nikki jumped in. "Mateo is busy this afternoon. He's got some work to do in his office, kiddo."

Mateo frowned at Nikki. She was pushing him out. It couldn't be clearer than it was at that moment.

No. He had to remind himself. She'd said herself that she wanted to spend time with her son. It was normal for a mother to want that—alone time with her boy. Mateo swallowed back the desire to ask her if he'd done something wrong. This was just his lack of self-confidence. Apparently, he hadn't gotten over what Caroline had done to him.

It begged the question: had there been signs? Had he missed something when he'd been with Caroline that would have tipped him off that she wasn't interested in him anymore?

Nikki's eyes flickered with pain, and she pulled her hands from his grasp with a sad smile. "We'll be back in time for me to prepare supper. It's just a nature walk."

Paxton skipped down the stairs, his boots thunking against them with each step he took. "Bye-bye, Mateo. See you soon."

Mateo turned, watching them exit out the front door. She hadn't even asked for her flowers. He hadn't gotten a chance to give them to her and tell her he loved her. Did she even care?

He shut his eyes just as the front door did. He couldn't allow his insecurities to get the better of him. He was better than that. *They* were better than that. People had bad days. He'd had one, hadn't he?

Mateo rolled his shoulders and blew out a calming breath. This was just a bump in the road. One bad day didn't mean anything in the grand scheme of things. He nodded more to himself than anything else.

Seeing Caroline today must have done a number on him. He was second-guessing everything. It wasn't fair to Nikki for him to overreact.

At least that was what he kept telling himself as he slipped back to his office. He had every intention of getting back to work, but that didn't happen. He ended up staring at the paperwork on his desk, unseeing, his thoughts shifting to the events that led him to this moment—the events that occurred nearly ten years ago.

He couldn't recall a single thing that could have clued him into Caroline's plans on their wedding day. There were no signs he could think of that he'd been blind enough to ignore. The way Nikki was behaving was nothing like the way Caroline had behaved. And yet he couldn't help but worry—not that Nikki was seeing someone else. He was worried she was pulling away and would end up choosing someone else over him.

23

———————

Nikki

$\mathcal{H}$e lied.

Mateo *actually* lied to her.

Nikki's whole body buzzed with frustration and an ache that she'd unsuccessfully attempted to bury. She'd seen him with Caroline. Why would he lie about it?

She wanted to believe that *if* he'd told her the truth right up front, she wouldn't have been hurt, but that would have been a lie. She knew it down to her toes that simply seeing them meet up had done something to her. It had shaken her so badly that she wasn't sure she'd be able to come back from it.

The irony of the whole situation was that she'd never been cheated on, but Mateo had. He should have known better than to keep something from her. They were together.

Unless they weren't.

Nikki looked up to the sky, the burning in her eyes

refusing to remain caged behind her lids. She couldn't cry right now. That wouldn't work—not when she was with Paxton. All he had to do was mention that she was sad to Mateo, and he'd come ask her what was wrong.

Then what?

She couldn't tell him that she knew he'd lied. If she did, he would think she was spying on him.

Technically, she had been. She'd stood there and watched them from the window without confronting them in the moment. Perhaps that had been her major mistake. Nikki should have marched into that coffee shop and demanded to know what was happening. Then, at least she wouldn't be walking along this trail while her son had the time of his life collecting leaves and interesting stones.

Never had she thought she could feel so down and alone before this moment. All she wanted to do was give up—tell Mateo to go after the girl he clearly liked.

Because that was the only thing that made sense.

She had to believe that Mateo wasn't trying to be deceptive to hurt her. He wasn't the type to get a thrill out of destroying others. No, this whole situation had to run deeper. On some level, Mateo likely still cared for Caroline. And why wouldn't he? They had been engaged. He'd proposed to her once. If she was throwing herself at him again, it wasn't a stretch to believe that he'd give her another chance.

A whimper slipped past her defenses, but thankfully her son didn't hear it. His boots crunched against the dirt and rocks that lined their path. Every few feet, he'd stoop to pick something up and place it in a small satchel he had at his waist. Paxton was completely oblivious to her pain and sorrow, and that was how it had to be.

As Nikki watched him, her heart sank even deeper into despair. Paxton had started to really care for Mateo. He'd opened up to the man after staying more reserved around Dennis. It had to have taken a lot of courage for him to let Mateo into his life.

Her steps slowed as the reality of it all settled on her. If Mateo left them for Caroline, he'd be hurting Paxton, too.

Her legs went weak. She'd sworn to herself that she wouldn't let Paxton become a casualty in her future relationships. Dennis hadn't wanted anything to do with him. He'd tolerated him, and they'd had some fun together, but he didn't want to adopt him or claim him as his own.

Nikki had been a fool to believe that Mateo had wanted something more with Paxton. And now her son would pay the price.

She was going to be sick. What had she done? She'd let her heart rule that logical side of her for too long. This wasn't just about her feelings. Mateo was messing with Paxton's too.

Her hands curled tightly into fists at her sides. She wasn't going to let that happen. If Mateo wanted to spend his time in the company of a woman who had destroyed him, that was his decision.

If he was going to keep it from her, then he could live with the repercussions that came from that dishonesty.

But in no way would she allow him to spend time with her son, getting closer to him and making him feel like there was a future with the three of them together.

Maybe it was time she found somewhere else to live.

Her stomach knotted so tightly she fought the instinct to gasp. Just the thought of trying to find something with the salary she had sounded like an impossible feat.

But as her gaze followed her son, she had to accept that was where they were at. It hadn't been smart to live under the same roof as Mateo in the first place. She brought her fingers up to her temples and rubbed them. Something told her that there would be a fight when she told Mateo her plans. He might not be firmly rooted in whatever relationship he had with her, but he was definitely stubborn.

"Are you okay, Mom?" Paxton's voice tore her to the present, and she opened her eyes to find him frowning up at her, a stone in his outstretched hand, apparently forgotten.

She pushed a smile to the surface and nodded. "I just have a headache. It'll go away after I get some rest."

Her son tilted his head, peering up at her with that gaze that could rip right past her defenses. "Do you want to go home?"

Nikki shook her head. "No. I promised you a nature walk, and that's what we're going to do."

He didn't look convinced. Her sweet boy was too aware for his own good. She took a step toward him and ruffled his hair. "Come on, kiddo. We're not even halfway there. You wanted to see the creek, right? It has the best rocks, from what I hear."

"I told you that." He laughed, scampering after her.

Nikki glanced over her shoulder at him and allowed herself the little bit of joy she had in watching him grow up. One day he wouldn't want to take nature walks with his mother. He'd find friends or a girlfriend, and he'd be too busy to entertain her. She couldn't let her fears and doubts over Mateo ruin these precious moments she had with her son.

She could feel his eyes on her as she brought the food out to the serving table. He wasn't in line for supper, but he was in the room. There, on the far side of the space, he leaned against the wall with arms crossed. Mateo hadn't moved from that spot since he'd arrived. She'd come out of the kitchen, taking three trips to get everything set out the way she liked. And each time, he'd been there.

Watching.

She refused to accept that he was feeling guilty over his meeting with Caroline. No, when she allowed herself to steal a look at him, she could read that much. If he wasn't feeling guilty, then what was it? Anger wasn't apparent, either. Nor was the joy she'd become so used to seeing. Something was up, but she couldn't figure it out—at least not from this distance.

Nikki wiped her hands on her apron and heaved a sigh. She'd avoided seeing him when she'd returned from her walk. Before she spoke to him, she had to figure out how she was going to break the news to him—that she wanted to move out.

Her job was important, and she could see a scenario where she ended up saying the wrong thing after he chose to leave her. Right now, she needed to prepare. She had to remain professional.

Pain rippled through her hands, and she stared down at them, finding that she was wringing them so tightly that they'd turned white. If she was honest with herself, she'd say she was scared—truly scared—that she wouldn't be able to follow through with her plan.

She spun on her heel, listening to the sounds of the hungry and appreciative cowboys getting their food. Nikki had insisted that Mark and Jason get their fill early so she could have their company in the back. Mateo might very well come back here to speak to her, and she needed any excuse she could find to not be alone with him.

Not today.

Swallowing the lump in her throat, she tossed a look at Mark, who was currently washing the dishes from the meal prep that had taken place. Jason was in the midst of putting what they didn't use into the fridge or the large pantry. Then he would set to work cleaning their counters and sweeping their floors. If she moved slowly enough, she'd have them shielding her for the remainder of the evening.

Mateo couldn't outlast her. Not if he wanted to get to bed at his usual time.

The kitchen door swung open, and Nikki wasn't the only one to glance in that direction.

"Oh, hey, boss. Can I get you something?" Jason paused his work.

Nikki dropped her attention to the binder she was working through. They'd have to put in another order soon, and she needed to make her list.

Mateo's eyes burned into the side of her face, but she refused to look up at him. If she did, she knew she wouldn't be strong enough not to crumble. She'd have to tell him what she saw. The fallout wasn't something she was prepared for.

Her face flushed as she continued going through the binder, her finger tracing down the page before her. She had to read the same thing three times before she glanced up at him again, hoping her expression was innocent enough to make him leave.

Mateo stared at her hard and then glanced at the others

in the kitchen briefly before turning to her again. "Dinner looks good."

Mark chuckled, not reading the room at all. "It tastes even better than it looks, boss."

Mateo cleared his throat, shuffled his feet, and rubbed the back of his neck. "Sophia was looking for you."

Nikki frowned. "She was?" What did Sophia need? They rarely spoke unless there was something important going on.

He nodded. "I think I saw her heading for the house. Maybe you should see what that's about before you head to bed."

She nodded, her stomach swirling. She wouldn't be leaving right now, though. That would open her up for a conversation she wasn't prepared to have—one where Mateo demanded answers. They stared at each other expectantly for a few moments until Mateo gave her a curt nod and strode from the kitchen.

Jason gave her a concerned look, but he knew better than to ask her what was going on. By now, most everyone on the premises knew that she and Mateo were an item. The last thing she wanted was for any of them to get involved in her relationship. The whole situation was messy enough as it was without people sticking their noses where they didn't belong.

Nikki forcibly turned her attention to the binder and let out a sigh of relief. It was clear she'd been avoiding Mateo all day today. And it was just as clear that he'd been trying to start up a conversation. What if he needed to tell her that they were breaking up, and she was just prolonging the inevitable?

She let a groan slip and dropped her elbows to the counter before placing her head in her hands.

"Everything alright, Nikki?" Jason asked quietly—so quiet that Mark must not have heard over the sound of the running water at the sink because he didn't stop his work.

"Yeah," she rasped. "Just peachy." Today wasn't a good day. Other than her little walk with Paxton, she didn't have anything good to show for it.

Trusting Caroline would be a mistake, but Nikki believed what she'd said. Caroline was interested in getting back together with her ex, and she was willing to do whatever it took to do so. Was Mateo on the same page?

That one was harder to tell.

"Well, if you need anything..." Jason mumbled.

She smiled and lifted her head, hoping she could reassure him enough that he didn't spread any rumors as to what might be happening. "Thanks. I appreciate it." Now she just had to deal with whatever it was Sophia wanted to discuss before she could hide away behind her bedroom door and finally get some peace.

24

———————

Mateo

"I don't know what to tell you, Mateo. She says she's fine."

"She's not," Mateo said, rubbing at his eyes. "Something is wrong, and it started on Friday last week." He hadn't gotten much sleep over the last week. Between Caroline attempting to reach out to him again and Nikki avoiding him like the plague, he couldn't seem to keep his head on straight.

Now, his work was suffering. He knew it was bad because Sophia had finally cornered him to ask him what was going on.

"If you don't believe me, go talk to her yourself," Sophia snapped.

He glanced over to her, finding her hands on her hips and that look of frustration on her face that said she meant business. The fact that she hadn't taken him by the ear and dragged him to Nikki herself was a surprise, to say the least. Mateo scowled at her. "You know I can't do that."

"Why not? She's *your* girlfriend."

"Because she won't talk to me. Any time I try to get her alone, she's either busy or she takes off. I'm telling you, something happened."

Sophia glanced at the building where Nikki worked as if that would give her the answer they were both looking for. "Maybe she's scared."

"Scared of what?" he practically shouted with exasperation. "I haven't done anything to scare her off. I got her flowers. That was it."

Sophia chewed on her lower lip. "I don't know."

Mateo was a bundle of nerves. The more he thought about it, the more he knew he was failing. The last time he'd been in a serious relationship, he'd been upfront and communicative, and that didn't work out well, either. Nikki wasn't Caroline. He really shouldn't be comparing the two of them to each other. If he were honest with himself, he would say that he cared for Nikki more than he had ever cared for Caroline. And perhaps that was the problem.

He was terrified of chasing her away. If she wasn't ready to talk to him about something, he needed to give her space.

But the voice in his head insisted that he was wrong. This wasn't a simple matter of miscommunication. He was trying. And she wanted space. He stifled a groan, prepared to finally ask Sophia for advice—something he'd told himself he would never do.

But her sharp tone cut him off.

"You have got to be kidding me. What is she doing here?"

His eyes snapped to a woman who had just climbed out of a sportscar.

No.

This couldn't be happening! What was she doing here?

Immediately, he looked toward the cafeteria. If Nikki saw her, it was over. He knew there was nothing going on with Caroline; they were no longer friends. But he also knew that Nikki had some severe self-confidence issues when it came to this vile woman. Without answering his sister's question, he darted forward, praying he would be able to get her to leave before his whole world officially imploded.

"Caroline," he gritted out when he was close enough. "What are you doing here?"

She smiled at him, her bright red lipstick stretching thinly across her face. A matching fingernail traced down his sternum. "I came to see you, silly."

He snatched her wrist and held it firmly. "You need to leave."

Caroline pouted. "You don't really mean that, do you?"

Mateo gritted his teeth, already hearing Sophia's approach from behind. His voice was a low growl as he glowered at Caroline. "You're not welcome here, which means you're trespassing. This is private property, and as such, I'm asking you to vacate the premises before I have to get the authorities involved."

She tilted her head, her eyes sparking. "This is about that other woman, isn't it?" Her focus shifted to scan the immediate area, but she didn't seem to find what she was looking for as she brought her gaze to lock with his again. "You're not going to get rid of me that easy."

"On the contrary, I think you will find it'll be easier than you expect." He released her wrist and took a step back. "I don't love you anymore."

"You don't love the person I was," she corrected him. "I've changed."

"I don't care."

Caroline strode closer and reached out to touch his face. Fire burned in his chest, the temptation to yank her hand behind her back and escort her to her car stronger than it had ever been. But he just stood there. She needed to see that she didn't affect him. Thankfully, his determination was working. She frowned at him and dropped her hand. "I'm going to prove it to you, Mateo. I'm going to show you exactly what you've been missing, and you're going to leave whoever that woman is for me. We belong together."

"Come on, you heard him. Leave," Sophia snapped, grabbing Caroline by the shoulders and spinning her around to push her toward her car. She threw a livid look at Mateo before she continued herding his ex back the way she'd come.

Mateo exhaled a sharp breath, feeling dirty for allowing her to even touch him. He watched her shuffle forward, heard her shrieks of protest when Sophia practically shoved her into her car. Caroline wasn't going to give up. It wasn't her style. She'd push and push until he had no more strength to push back. Then she'd slither under his defenses and tear him apart from the inside.

Slowly, he glanced toward the cafeteria, wishing he could just go to Nikki and hold her in his arms. He needed her strength and her humor. He needed reassurance that they were going to be okay.

Sophia shoved his shoulder so hard he stumbled back a step, his boot snagging on a rock before he tumbled to the dirt. He glowered up at her, the dust cloud around him permeating his senses.

"What was that for?" he snapped.

She stood above him, her eyes flashing with wild fury. "What were you thinking?"

He winced as he dusted the dirt from his hands and climbed to his feet. "What do you mean? I didn't do anything."

Sophia's arm shot out, pointing a finger where Caroline had been parked. "Why would you let her come here?"

This time he focused on dusting his backside from the dirt that clung to it. "It's a free country, Sophia," he gritted out. "What did you want me to do? File for a restraining order?"

"Yes!"

His eyes snapped to meet hers before he released a baffled and yet jaded laugh. "You realize you can only request them after recorded conflicts have already taken place, right? She would have had to damage our property or hurt someone—"

"She hurt *you*! Or did you forget that when she had her hands all over you?"

He glowered at her. "She didn't have her hands all over me," Mateo said sheepishly.

Sophia scoffed. "From my vantage point, it didn't look like you were bothered all that much by the way she was treating you. I wonder what Nikki might have thought if she caught you two together like that."

A terrifying chill coursed down his spine. They were in a strong enough relationship that Nikki would have given him the benefit of the doubt, right? She would have asked him what was going on, and he would have told her. Part of him wished she had been out here with them when Caroline showed up. At least then she would have heard him tell Caroline to leave.

"How long has she been in town? Please tell me that she's visiting friends or something and happened to find out we live here."

Mateo dragged his hand down his face and groaned. "It's not a secret that we moved here, Sophia. It's all over our social media pages. It wouldn't take a sleuth to figure out where we live."

"So, she just shows up out of the blue? Nah. I don't believe that for a second. She had to have reached out first."

He avoided looking at her, and that was all it took for Sophia to put together some very important pieces.

"Mateo!" she hissed. "Please tell me you haven't been speaking with her."

Still, he didn't respond. He should never have let her talk him into coffee.

"Are you kidding me?" Sophia paced in front of him, running her hands through her hair as her face tinted colors. "How many times, Mateo?"

"What?"

"How long have you been going behind Nikki's back—"

"I didn't go behind her back," he growled, prowling toward her. "I bumped into that lunatic in town, and she wanted to get coffee. That's it."

"*That's it*," she muttered sardonically. She threw her hands into the air. "Sometimes I don't even know whether or not you care for Nikki or if it's just—"

His hand reached out lightning fast, and he took her wrist in his grasp. "Don't you dare finish that sentence."

Sophia's face twisted with disgust as she dragged her hand from his.

"*Of course,* I care about her. I care about her... a lot." He nearly told his sister he was in love, but this wasn't the time for that. Caroline's presence and his sister's accusations had soured the possibility for any sort of confession of love. "I don't know why Caroline is showing up out of the blue. She must have figured out that we live here and she was in town, so she decided to... I don't know." He groaned. "She wants me back."

Sophia snorted. "Of course she does. Because she's a worm, and you're... everything."

He gave her a wry look.

"What?" she snapped. "You're on a completely different level than her, and you know it. She doesn't deserve the dirt beneath your feet."

Mateo rubbed the back of his neck and glanced away. "Thanks," he mumbled.

"I guess there's one thing we can be grateful for."

"What's that?"

"Nikki didn't see Caroline stop by. And all of Caroline's feeble attempts to get you back? She didn't see that either. We just have to make sure Caroline understands that she isn't getting you back. She lost you when she chose that other guy, and there is no changing it."

"I don't think it's going to be as easy as you think. Caroline is the type of person to go after what she wants even if the odds are stacked against her. She's not going to give up until she gets me or destroys my life in the process."

Sophia frowned contemplatively at him. "Then we have to make sure that doesn't happen. Whatever is going on with Nikki—we need to fix it so you guys are strong."

"That's just it, though. How am I supposed to fix it if Nikki won't tell me what's wrong? Maybe this is all for nothing. Maybe I'm just going to be a bachelor for the rest of my life."

Sophia snorted. "You're not going to be a bachelor for the rest of your life. If it doesn't work out with Nikki—"

"I don't want anyone else, Sophia," he said in a whisper, but he knew she heard him based on the way her eyes widened and lips parted.

"Well, I guess you're just gonna have to hang in there. The good thing is that Nikki hasn't spoken to Caroline in ages. She said so herself. So that means she won't know what Caroline is up to."

He could tell by the sound of her voice that Sophia was trying to cheer him up. Maybe she felt guilty about how she'd reacted. Or maybe she could see the anguish he was dealing with. Mateo nodded and glanced once more toward the cafeteria building. "Yeah. You're probably right."

Sophia reached out to touch his arm, her voice quiet. "I'll keep trying to talk to Nikki. If something is actually wrong, I'll get it out of her."

"Thanks, *really*," he repeated from before.

"What are sisters for?"

25

Nikki

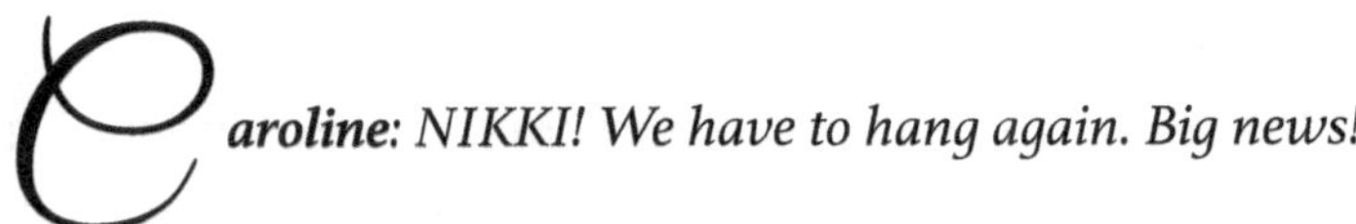

aroline: NIKKI! We have to hang again. Big news!

NIKKI CLUTCHED her phone as she read the message that had just come through her social media account. She could almost imagine the glass shattering beneath the force as she scowled at the message. There was only one reason why Caroline would send that. Something had happened between herself and Mateo.

Unless she was lying.

Nikki didn't dare hope. She refused to lose herself in the disappointment that her relationship with Mateo had become.

After a week of avoiding him, she'd managed to convince herself to spend time with him—mostly because Paxton had insisted that she needed to see how good he'd gotten in the saddle.

Her son had been right. He was a natural if there ever was one, and he'd be so disappointed when he found out that they'd have to move from this place and find a small apartment above a store or something.

She lifted her eyes to her son, ignoring the message as she shoved the phone into her pocket. As if against her will, her focus drifted to Mateo. Everything was still strained. She knew he could tell she wasn't happy, and she hated herself for it. He deserved better.

She deserved better.

A sigh fell from her lips, and she found herself wishing she could just go up to him and tell him that they were over. It would solve so many problems. He'd have his freedom, and she wouldn't have to wait for the other shoe to drop.

Her phone felt heavy in her pocket, demanding her attention. If Caroline had news, and she was being honest, that meant Mateo was still keeping things from her. Nikki could just ask Caroline what her news was. But what would she tell Mateo?

Hey, you know how I told you that I wasn't on speaking terms with your ex-fiancée? Well, we're hanging out now. Hope you don't mind.

Nikki grimaced. That wouldn't go over well at all.

She placed a hand on her stomach, attempting to quell the nerves. Nikki already knew what was going to happen. She wasn't going to be able to stop herself. She'd speak to Caroline again despite the fact that the woman was utter poison. It was the only way she could figure out exactly what was going on between Mateo and Caroline, and then she'd confront him.

That rolling and twisting in her stomach thrashed even more at the thought of that conversation. It needed to happen. She couldn't avoid Mateo forever. She needed closure, and since he hadn't told her he wanted to break things off, it would be up to her.

Nikki's eyes found Mateo once more, and he offered her that adorable, crooked grin. Her heart crumbled at the sight of it. How was she going to let go of the one good thing she'd found?

He stopped Paxton's ride for a moment, and they spoke in hushed tones. Mateo glanced over at her before saying something more and letting him continue. She watched as he headed straight for her.

Oh no. This was it. He was going to break things off, and she wouldn't even have to speak to Caroline at all.

Mateo stood beside her, his arm brushing against hers. She craved his touch more than she wanted to admit. She wanted him to reach for her hand, to slip his arm around her waist and pull her toward him. She wanted him to show her how much he cared. But she'd been so cold lately. How could she expect him to do any of that?

He took off his hat and ran a hand through his hair, his eyes remaining locked on her son. "He's doing well."

"He has a good teacher," she said.

One side of his mouth quirked upward. "You can't beat natural talent."

She nodded, shifting her feet in the dirt. They stood there in awkward silence for a few moments, and then Mateo sighed.

"I get that you're going through something."

Nikki stiffened.

"But I want you to know that I'm here for you if you want to talk."

Right here. She could tell him right now that she wanted to talk about him seeing two women or at least entertaining it. She could demand answers.

But one look at her son, and she knew she couldn't do that to him. She didn't want to fight. She just wanted peace.

Nikki drew in a deep breath and glanced at him out of the corner of her eye. "Yeah, thanks."

"Nikki—"

She cut him off. "I might have to run an errand later today or tomorrow. Do you think you could keep an eye on Paxton for me?" She really shouldn't have asked him—especially since he might not be in Paxton's life for much longer. Well, maybe she'd still want him to teach Paxton how to handle a horse while she worked here. Things would be different, though.

"Sure." His voice tore her from her musings, and she eyed him once more.

"Thank you," she whispered.

"I'd do anything for you, Nikki." There was something about his tone that struck her at her core. It wasn't exactly a goodbye, but there was resignation in it—as if he was preparing for their relationship to come to an end.

And with that realization, the rest of her heart fractured. She bit down hard, willing the tears to remain behind her eyes. She couldn't break here. Not right now in front of Paxton. All she could do was nod.

"Where are you going? Want me to tag along?"

Nikki's heart leaped into her throat as Sophia managed to come out of nowhere. She jumped and gaped at Sophia for a bit too long, her face flushing with embarrassment as she caught sight of Sophia staring at her with curiosity.

"You okay?" Sophia asked.

Nikki nodded. She wasn't doing anything wrong. She was meeting up with a friend. No, not a friend. She was meeting up with Caroline to tell her once and for all to leave her alone. And if she got that tidbit of information that Mateo might be hiding from her, she could wash her hands of the whole situation once and for all. "I'm fine," she rasped out, her hand on her chest. It still thundered, but due to being surprised or out of fear she'd get caught, she couldn't be certain. "I'm just heading to town for a bit."

"Want some company?"

Nikki practically choked out the words, "No, thanks. I just want... to be alone." Lies. All of them. What she wouldn't give to have Sophia at her side to tell Caroline off if she got too mouthy.

Sophia frowned, then stepped closer and lowered her voice. "Whatever it is that's bothering you—holding you back—I want you to know one thing."

Nikki itched to run. She didn't want to be part of this conversation. She needed out. But Sophia's hand on her arm kept her feet planted.

"You and Mateo? You're the endgame, okay? That isn't to say that times won't get tough. I can't tell you how often I've seen evidence of people losing out on something good just because they let something important fall through the cracks."

Important.

Like honesty.

Who was she to judge, though? She hadn't exactly been honest about what she was feeling. She hadn't admitted to seeing him with Caroline. And she hadn't asked him if he was having second thoughts about their own relationship.

The guilt was eating at her more these days. Even if she chose to turn around and speak to Mateo instead of going to visit with Caroline, she wasn't sure she could say what needed to be said without at least finishing what she needed to with the woman who wanted to come between them.

Nikki did the only thing she could. She threw her arms around Sophia and whispered, "Thanks."

Sophia pulled back and smiled. "Let me know if you ever need to talk about anything. And I'll be here."

Nikki nodded.

THE RESTAURANT WAS busy for a Saturday afternoon. Caroline had found them a booth, and she was already drinking a fruity cocktail. The second she saw Nikki, she waved her over with a shout. "There you are! I'm so glad you made it."

Nikki paused near the hostess's podium. Her gut was telling her to leave. She needed to speak to Mateo and work out her issues with him, not Caroline.

But the two of them had problems too—problems that Caroline was totally blind to.

Nikki took a steadying breath and headed for the booth. She slid across from Caroline and put her purse at her side. "We need to talk."

"Oh, don't I know it." Caroline took a long swig of her

drink and leaned forward conspiratorially. "I saw Mateo again."

Nikki's voice died in her throat. She'd been prepared to tell her ex-best friend that she was seeing Mateo, and Caroline needed to stay away. She'd pumped herself up enough to have the courage to tell the woman in front of her that she didn't deserve to have Mateo again and had lost her chance. Last of all, she had planned on telling her to leave them both alone and find her own life.

But now?

Now, she was that shattered little girl that Caroline pushed around in high school all over again. The little girl who Caroline said would never find a guy because she wasn't good enough. That little girl who had started to believe every veiled, derogatory comment that came from those perfect red lips.

Nikki blinked. "You did."

Caroline nodded. "He was so sweet. You could tell he wanted to kiss me, but his sister was there."

Sophia? Was she in on this too?

Suddenly, Caroline's happy expression shifted to one of concern. Her brows pulled together, and she pouted. "Oh. That's right. You had a crush on him once, didn't you?"

Nikki was numb. She couldn't move. Of course, Caroline would remember that.

She reached forward and patted Nikki's hand. "It's okay to be disappointed. He was totally out of your league anyway. He needs someone who can stand next to him—to be part of a power couple. Someone who can bring him to home plate. And you?" Her eyes trailed over Nikki with a flicker of disdain. "You're out in left field, sweetie. He'd never want someone like you, anyway."

The confession was in her throat at that moment. She wanted to tell Caroline that they were together. Mateo cared for her, not Caroline. But her doubts restrained her. Maybe Caroline was right.

"No," Nikki mumbled, shaking her head.

"You say something?"

Nikki glowered at Caroline. "You're wrong. Mateo is nothing like you. He's kind and sweet, and he doesn't care about that sort of thing. We're dating."

Caroline snorted a laugh. "Oh, *sweetheart*. Is that what he told you?"

Nikki clenched her hands into fists, hating the way Caroline was speaking to her.

Her lower lip protruded again, and she shook her head with a cluck of her tongue. "Normally, I'd be jealous that he spent time with you. But what I really feel is pity."

Pity?

Caroline sighed. "Don't feel dumb, Nikki. We can all fall for the lies of someone when they're good at weaving them. Don't you see it? We're both being played. Me, because he's trying to make me jealous. You because..." Her eyes trailed up and down her frame again. "Well, you get what I'm saying."

Nikki couldn't believe it. She wouldn't believe it. Mateo was nothing like Caroline. He was *good*.

And yet he'd lied.

Twice.

That lump returned to her throat. How could she believe Mateo when she'd seen with her own eyes that they'd spent time together?

"Here, let me get you a drink. You look like you need one." Caroline edged out of her seat and headed straight for the bar, leaving Nikki to drown in her despair. Within a few seconds, someone settled into Caroline's vacant spot.

Slowly, Nikki lifted her eyes and stared at a handsome cowboy. His sleeves were short enough to show off his muscular form. He had a charming smile, and he pushed a drink toward her. He must work at the bar.

Her thoughts were confirmed when he cocked his head and said, "This one is on the house. Your friend said you were in need of a pick-me-up."

Nikki offered him a small smile, accepting the glass. Her fingers accidentally brushed his, and she snapped back. "Sorry."

"No worries, darlin'. Let me know if you need anything else." He winked at her, but it did nothing. All Nikki could think about was Mateo's smile, the way he smelled, and the way she felt when he touched her.

Nikki stared at the drink, frowning at its contents. She needed to get back home. She couldn't just stay here and let Caroline drag her into the depths of her own personal purgatory. She needed to talk to Mateo. Either they were going to work this out or they were going to be over. One way or another, she'd have her answer.

26

Mateo

ateo's world was crashing down around him. This couldn't be happening.

Not again.

He squeezed his eyes shut, an all-familiar numbness taking hold of his heart. No, he wasn't numb. He was cold. His body had chilled from the inside out, and it felt like ice crystals were starting to fracture within his very soul.

Opening his eyes again, he stared at his phone's screen.

Nikki was smiling. She was staring into the eyes of some stranger at a restaurant. The table had been set for two. It was a date.

His hand tightened on the device, and for a moment, he thought he might crack the screen with the strength of his grasp. With controlled fury, he placed the phone screen down on the counter.

Not again.

Why her?

She knew how this would affect him. She'd seen the trauma he'd had to overcome when Caroline had chosen another.

"Mateo?"

His head snapped around to find Paxton standing in the doorway, a worried crease between his brows. "Are you mad?"

His small, timid voice had Mateo's heart lurching. Nikki hadn't said anything to make him believe that her ex had been abusive. There was no reason for Paxton to be worried just because Mateo felt like everything was shattering around him. And yet, the look on that boy's face had Mateo wondering just how little Nikki's ex had cared for the boy.

As much as it pained Mateo, he put a smile on his face. "I'm sorry, bud. I got distracted." He was supposed to be getting them popcorn for their movie. "You don't want to miss any of the show. I'll be right there."

Paxton's frown didn't leave his face. He was smart. That kid clearly knew something was up, and it wouldn't take long for him to bring it up to his mother.

A twist of pain wrapped around Mateo's middle.

He couldn't believe he was in this situation again. How could he have been so stupid as to allow himself to repeat the past?

Mateo watched the kid retreat, and he blew out a sigh as he laced his fingers atop his head and paced the kitchen. Maybe he was overreacting. The message didn't exactly come from a reputable source.

Then again, Caroline had no reason to send it to him except to rub it in his face that the girl he was madly in love with was breaking his heart just like Caroline had.

His despair surged into fury. How she'd managed to discover that he was seeing Nikki wasn't clear. He didn't want to believe that Nikki had been lying about that, too. Maybe they had been in contact with one another.

Fingers wrapping around the counter to steady himself, Mateo sucked in a deep breath and told himself to focus. She'd said she was running errands. Sophia had said she wanted to be alone.

And yet he had photographic proof that neither one of those statements was true.

Even if the picture didn't accurately tell the whole story, Nikki had lied.

She'd have a lot of explaining to do when she returned home.

A CAR DOOR SLAMMED SHUT, and Mateo stiffened. Beside him, Paxton sat on the couch with a giant bowl of popcorn that he'd barely touched. Neither one of them had been interested in chowing down. Mateo got the sense that Paxton could feel something was off. He'd been too quiet.

Did he know?

Had Nikki introduced him to that man in the picture?

Mateo's hand curled into a fist, and he shut his eyes again before exhaling. "Hey, bud. I think your mom's back. You keep watching the movie. It's almost over."

Paxton turned his face upward, that worried frown still marring his features. "Okay."

Mateo flashed him a smile he hoped didn't look as pained as he felt, and he ruffled the boy's hair.

His heart thrashed with each step he took toward the

door. His breathing was uneven, and it almost felt like he could crumble right there on the porch as she moved toward him. She stopped a few feet short of the steps, her eyes connecting with his.

Guilt.

He could see it in her eyes. The way they shuddered with the weight of a secret she didn't want him to discover only made his gut churn. This had to be the worst possible betrayal she could have come up with.

And it hurt even more because of their past.

Mateo's jaw flexed as he gripped the banister with both hands. Wood creaked beneath his hold of the railing. He didn't want to think about the photo or the words Caroline had sent with them.

I told you I was the better fit. At least with me, you know what you're getting into.

He took in a deep breath through his nose. Nikki and he were at a standoff. He wasn't even sure if she'd be brave enough to come another step closer. The blood had quickly drained from Nikki's face, and that was all the proof he needed to know she knew she'd been caught.

Maybe he was just a glutton for punishment. Because he needed to hear it from her own lips.

"How did your *errands* go?" he sniped.

She flinched and dropped her focus to her hands. "Mateo—"

"Tell me something, Nikki." He pushed away from where he stood and headed down the stairs, not caring that his voice sounded entirely too sinister. "Why are you pulling away from me?"

Her head snapped up, and it momentarily threw him off to see the surprise in her eyes. "I'm not—"

"Yes, you are," he bit out.

Nikki's eyes narrowed to slits, and the guilt was completely overshadowed by a sharp, accusatory look. She folded her arms as the rate of her breathing increased. "If I pulled away, it's because you *lied*."

"*I* lied? That's rich, coming from you." He released a mirthless laugh and spun around to pace just like he had in the kitchen. He completely disregarded the fact that she thought he was capable of that sort of deception. "I can't believe I allowed myself to give in to the fairytale." He muttered it more to himself than anyone else. "I should have known that honest relationships are practically impossible to find."

"You want to talk about *honest*? I'll give you honest," she snapped, dragging him back to the present. "From the very beginning, I knew that you didn't want me. Not really."

His head whipped around so fast that he might have pulled something. What was she talking about? He'd been the one to seek her out. He'd been the one to fall first. He was the one with a shattered heart in his chest. Before he could lash out at her over everything he'd just seen, she cut him off.

Nikki waved a hand down herself. "You can't tell me this is your first choice. I know I'm not the standard for beauty, but I guess it was too easy to get me to believe that you might want something different after spending your life dating shallow, stick-thin women like Caroline."

"What are you *talking* about?" he blurted.

She rolled her eyes and let out a strangled huff. "Seriously? How long have we known each other? Have you forgotten that I've seen the girls you dated in high school? My best friend was the one you *proposed* to. You might not want to admit it, but you definitely had a type, and these curves? They don't fit in that perfect little box, do they?"

His bewilderment was almost enough to distract him from the real issue at hand. "You think that I'm not attracted to you?" He'd given her no indication he felt any such thing. Where was her evidence? Mateo took a step toward her, frustrated beyond belief. "Nikki—"

Her hand flew up between them, warding him off. "No. I get it now. I understand. This thing between us was a fling. It was nice while it lasted, but when—" Her eyes widened momentarily, and she looked away.

"When what, Nikki? What were you going to say?"

She wrapped her arms around herself and shook her head. "You know what? It doesn't matter."

"Yes, it does," he seethed, his fury returning. "Because everything you've been telling yourself is a lie. Whatever it is you think is going on, it's not true."

She still glowered at him, shaking her head. "I thought you knew better. With your history? I thought you would have learned something."

His mouth fell open. "What is that supposed to mean?"

Her lips pressed into a thin line. He wanted to shake the truth out of her. He wanted her to tell him what made her believe he'd done something so terrible that she'd go on a date with another guy. His hands shook as that picture filled his mind. He'd never considered himself a jealous guy. Heck, if Caroline had sent him a message without proof, he wouldn't have believed it. Even after that woman had blown his world to pieces, he'd been willing to trust again.

He'd been an idiot.

"You don't know what you're talking about," he hissed, dragging his phone from his pocket. "I would never hurt you.

I would never lie to you. But this? Apparently, women are just made for betrayal." He shoved the phone at her.

Nikki fumbled with it a moment, and then her eyes lowered to the screen. The words from Caroline were right above the picture of Nikki with the man Mateo didn't know. She stared at the picture for a long moment, time slowing as all the pieces came together. When she lifted her eyes, tears lined her lashes. Without a word, she shoved the phone right back into his chest and stormed into the house.

That was it. No explanation. No attempts to clear her name.

Caroline had been right.

He lost track of time as he stood there. His limbs refused to operate the way they used to. That numbness returned full force. What had he expected? That she'd drop to his feet and plead for him to forgive her?

Fire prickled behind his eyes, and he dug his fingernails into his hands. He wasn't going to cry over this. When Caroline had turned his life inside out, he'd told himself he wouldn't blindly trust anyone. That was why it had taken him ten years to finally be willing to open his heart. The fact that Nikki had managed to get past his defenses only showed what a fool he still was.

"Hey, what are you doing out here? Weren't you supposed to be hanging with Paxton today?"

Sophia's voice filtered to his ears past the raging thoughts that spun tumultuously in his head. Slowly, his eyes shifted to her, finding concern laced in their depths.

"Yeah," his voice cracked. "But Nikki is back, so..."

She nodded. "Okay. And why does it look like you've been hit by a bus?"

He sucked in a deep inhale, feeling like his lungs were screaming for air. "Maybe because it feels like I have."

"What's going on?" she said.

When he didn't answer, she grabbed his upper arm and pulled him back to the steps to sit down.

"Mateo, what's wrong?" Sophia prodded again. "Did something happen with the ranch? With Nikki?"

"It's over, Sophia," he rasped, not trusting his voice. "We're over." He placed his head in his hands and fought the temptation to completely disintegrate in front of his sister. She'd been there after Caroline. She'd witnessed him breaking and had helped him put the pieces back together. He couldn't make her do that again. "You were right," he whispered, not looking at her. "I should have never dated someone who works for me."

"I don't think I ever said that," she said softly.

"Doesn't matter." He hated how his voice shook. "Because it's true. It's going to be torture having her here, not being able to touch her—hold her." *Love her.*

Except he'd keep on loving her. He knew he would, which was why he understood on a much deeper level that he wouldn't be able to survive this one. He loved Nikki— more than he'd loved Caroline even. And seeing her every day, living under the same roof as her—already his heart was withering up and dying inside.

"What happened?" Sophia placed a hand on his back. "Whatever it is, I'm sure it's just a big misunderstanding. Communication is really important, Mateo—"

"Don't you think I know that?" His whole body stiffened, and she gasped at the movement. Mateo glared at his sister. "I learned that lesson a long time ago. I know how important it is to talk and get the truth out. I tried. I asked her to come clean before I accused her of…"

Sophia's eyes bounced from one of his eyes to the other as she searched his face, waiting for the answers. He couldn't tell her. Not the whole truth. She'd hate Nikki for it. Their friendship would suffer. Then who would Nikki have to turn to?

Even after what she'd done, he couldn't do that to her.

Mateo took a deep breath and shook his head before getting to his feet. "She doesn't want me, Sophia. And you can't force someone to love you no matter how much you might love them first."

"Mateo—"

"Drop it, okay? I'm an adult. We'll be cordial. It's not like I'm going to kick her out or fire her. I should have known better, and now I can suffer the consequences."

"Mateo—" she tried again, but he ignored her and headed for the barn. He needed to get out of there. He needed to clear his head and figure out his next steps. One thing was for certain, he wasn't going to reply to Caroline. That message had been clear. She was gloating. She wanted to rub salt in the wound after she'd sliced him open.

The worst part was that she'd finally taught him a lesson he should have already learned.

Trust was an imaginary concept—one he'd never fully obtain.

27

———————

Nikki

ikki could have been a ghost floating through the house for how she felt. Nothing felt solid anymore. She couldn't breathe. She couldn't even hear the thump, thump of her heart anymore.

She wanted to be mad. She had wanted to throw Mateo's phone at him and demand that he ask her who the guy was and why she was sitting with him, but she couldn't. The second she saw who the message had come from, she'd lost her will to fight.

Mateo had lied about Caroline—about seeing her, about giving her flowers.

Not only that, but he had also been in contact with her even when he insisted he didn't want anything to do with her. He wouldn't even talk about her when Nikki tried to bring her up. It was as if Mateo had compartmentalized everything in his life.

The person he was with Nikki wasn't the man who still held feelings for Caroline.

She didn't know how she managed to get to her room without stumbling or falling down the stairs. Thankfully, Paxton appeared to be engrossed enough in the movie he was watching that he hadn't seemed to notice her slip by the living room.

Nikki needed to think. She needed to regroup. Meeting Caroline had backfired so miserably that there was no coming back from it. That much was clear. Not only had Caroline figured out how to get to Mateo, but she'd also managed to make Mateo believe that Nikki wasn't worth his time.

A sob racked her body as she crumpled against the door and slid to the ground. The lies and deception had become too much. It probably wouldn't have even helped if she'd told Mateo or Sophia where she was going today. Based on everything she'd experienced, Mateo had already been long gone.

So what was the point in any of it? Why should she explain that the man who sat across from her at the table had only been the bartender, and he'd only been wanting to check on her? Why should she admit to visiting with Caroline if only to tell her to back off?

None of it would have changed the outcome of their argument. They'd been on the path to destruction from the moment Mateo had lied about visiting with Caroline at that coffee shop.

A knock sounded at the door to her back and Nikki gasped, quieting her sobs. She couldn't bring herself to talk to him, to see him. She didn't want him to know how much his betrayal had hurt her. The next several weeks were already going to be the worst of her life. She'd have to find another job. She'd have to get a new place to stay. She'd been saving every spare penny she had from working here, so maybe she had enough to pay for rent, but what about furnishings and food? Those had been included in this position. If she left, would she end up back where she started from? With nothing?

Another knock, then Sophia's voice came through the door. "Nikki? You okay?"

Panic swirled around Nikki like a tornado. Had she talked to Mateo? Of course, she had. Those two were the closest out of the siblings. And if Nikki knew them like she thought she did, there was zero chance that Mateo kept the picture from Sophia.

But if that was true, Sophia wouldn't sound as concerned, would she? Where was the anger? The accusation? Where was the sister who stuck up for her brother to the point where she wouldn't think twice about kicking Nikki to the curb?

Was it Paxton?

Sophia wouldn't kick Nikki out if it meant Paxton would suffer.

Nikki closed her eyes and took a deep breath before wiping at her face with her fingertips. "I'm fine," she called out shakily.

"No, you're not," she said through the door. "I heard you crying."

"Yeah, well," Nikki said and let out a blubbering laugh, "maybe they're happy tears."

Sophia sighed. "I'm coming in."

Nikki stiffened, pressing her back to the door. "No. I don't want you to."

"Nikki, whatever it is, you need to talk about it. Mateo is upset too. So maybe the two of you just need to cool off and talk some more later."

She shook her head even though Sophia had no chance of seeing it. "There's nothing to talk about."

Sophia attempted to push the door open. "Nikki, I mean it. Let me in. Whatever happened, we can figure it out."

"What if I don't want to figure it out?" Nikki felt like she'd shattered into a thousand pieces. The thought of picking through each one was about as appealing as picking through shards of broken glass. She didn't want to be comforted. She didn't need assurances that everything was going to be okay because it wasn't. There was no coming back from this. They were each guilty of deception, and neither one of them had the strength to get through it alone. "It's better this way," she grunted as Sophia really put her shoulder into her attempts at entering the room.

"We might not have been close in high school, but we're close now. And if you think I'm going to let you sit in here and pretend that you're not broken up about whatever happened, then you don't know me at all."

The door pushed at Nikki's back again and again as Sophia continued her attempts at entry. There was no running from this. Nikki could let her in now, or she could get cornered by Sophia later. She might as well get it over with when her wounds were open and bleeding rather than tearing them open to let them fester down the road.

"Fine," she snapped.

The door stilled. "You're going to let me in?"

Nikki brushed at her wet face again. "Yeah. Just... wait a sec, okay?" She got to her feet and moved over to her dresser before pulling out some makeup wipes so she could swipe them over her cheeks. She wasn't even sure she was prepared to talk to Sophia about why the argument had started in the first place. Sophia had indicated on more than one occasion how much she hated Caroline, and Nikki didn't want to be the reason a rift came between the two siblings.

She took a deep, unsettled breath, then called out, "You can come in."

Sophia pushed the door open. The hesitant way she did was almost humorous compared to how insistent she'd been on entering only seconds ago. Her eyes connected with Nikki, and she sighed. "What did he do?"

A sad laugh bubbled out of Nikki's chest, and she shook her head. "What makes you think it was him?"

Sophia pushed the door shut with her back, then placed her hands on her hips. "Because I know you."

"And he's your brother."

Her friend shrugged. "I guess I figure that guys have a tendency to be dumber when it comes to relationships."

Nikki winced. They both knew that wasn't a correct statement when it came to Caroline. And now, Nikki could be thrown into that net as well.

"Hey," Sophia said, softer this time, moving forward. "What happened? He wouldn't tell me. He just said it was over."

A fresh slice of sharp pain dragged through Nikki. It was unexpected. Hadn't Nikki realized it was over the second she walked away from Mateo? Wasn't she already planning on leaving the ranch in search of a new job and a place to live?

Even still, the heavy ache that came from Sophia's words stole the breath from her lungs.

Sophia pulled Nikki in for a hug. "Tell me what he did,

and I'll make sure he apologizes. Then we can get the two of you back on track."

Nikki shook her head, tears already starting to spill. "There's no going back. He doesn't want me. And why would he? I'm not exactly the kind of girl—"

Sophia pushed her back but kept her hands clutching at Nikki's upper arms. "What? He didn't say that."

It was hard to maintain the searching stare that Sophia kept her pinned with. The urge to tear herself away from her friend and demand that she leave was more than crushing. But Nikki stood firm. "Technically..." she hedged.

Sophia frowned. "I know he wouldn't say that. Nikki, no one has made him as happy as you have. I've seen it. The last ten years? He was a shell of himself. When he was with Caroline, he wasn't as happy as he has been with you. And I'm not just saying that because you're my favorite person. I'm saying that because I can tell you're good for him." She gave Nikki a little shake. "Whatever is happening isn't the end. You have to believe that."

Nikki wanted to tell her. She wanted to spill all of Mateo's secrets—that he'd been speaking to Caroline. That he'd been sneaking around to see her. But she couldn't. That would make her a hypocrite for doing the exact same thing. She shut her eyes, letting the pooling tears fall. "We're not good for each other, Sophia. We're just... not. He wants something else, and I'm not going to stand in his way. He can have her back. It's clearly what he wants."

Sophia's eyes narrowed and she opened her mouth, but someone downstairs hollered her name. At first, all she did was turn her head to the door. Then she turned back to Nikki, but they called for her again. She let out a sigh. "I'm going to see what that is all about, and then we're going to continue this conversation."

Nikki shook her head. "Just drop it, okay? If you care for me and your brother, you won't meddle in what's going on. Let things end the way they are. It's already too messy, and I don't want you to get caught up in the middle of it."

A look of pain crossed over Sophia's features as she pulled away. Then she sighed and nodded. "Fine. But if you decide you want to talk about it—"

"I know," Nikki whispered. "Thanks, Sophia."

28

Mateo

Every. Single. Time.

Mateo's eyes followed Nikki as she strode across the property toward the building where she spent most of her time. He could sense her before he saw her. And every time he did, he'd turn, and he couldn't tear his eyes from her.

Even after he knew she'd gone behind his back to have lunch with some random guy, he couldn't make himself hate her.

He rubbed his fist over the place where his heart used to be. In its place was probably a shriveled up organ that couldn't pass for anything. His soul ached. There was a piece of him missing now.

The worst part was that the more he thought about it, the more things weren't adding up. Nikki didn't go anywhere frequently enough to be seeing someone. And he would have heard if someone came here to see her. He'd asked

Paxton some vague questions about his mother, and the boy had answered innocently enough.

There was simply no evidence that she was interested in dating.

But he'd seen the picture. Caroline might have been vile, but she wasn't good enough to photoshop a picture of Nikki with someone else. And Nikki had come home wearing the same clothes that she'd been wearing in that picture.

He'd pulled it out several times to try to make sense of it. At one point, he'd nearly messaged Caroline to demand more information. Why was she at the same place Nikki had been? And how had she known that he was dating Nikki? Sending him the picture had been a calculated decision on her part.

"You need to stop obsessing," Daniel said at his side. "The two of you broke things off a week ago."

And yet, Caroline continued to reach out. She'd extended her trip, too. On top of all that, she'd asked several different times if she could help Mateo forget about Nikki.

Mateo dragged a hand down his face and finally met his friend's eyes. "I'm not obsessing."

Daniel laughed. "You definitely are." He jerked a chin toward the building where Nikki had disappeared. "I don't get it. You two ended things. It was mutual. So why are you acting like she's the one who broke things off with you?"

He hadn't been able to bring himself to tell Daniel about the picture. And while he'd been immensely curious about why Nikki thought he was lying to her, he wasn't willing to confront her about that aspect either. It was better this way —to leave things the way they were.

"There's something you're not telling me, isn't there?" Daniel said.

Mateo scowled at Daniel. "If I'm not telling you something, then it's clearly none of your business."

Daniel lifted both hands with a smirk. "All I'm saying is that if you want to talk about it, I won't breathe a word to anyone. Not to Aria, not to Sophia... no one. Maybe there's something you're missing."

His friend was starting to sound like the echoes in his head. Nothing about this breakup felt right. Sure, they'd hashed things out. She didn't feel loved, and he couldn't trust her. Both of those things were necessary in a relationship.

He sighed again and raked his hand down his face. "Fine."

Daniel's brows lifted.

"You heard about my ex, right?"

"The witch who cheated on you and left you at the altar?"

Mateo flinched. The way Daniel could say it so easily still cut. "Yeah, that one."

"What about her?"

"You know she was Nikki's best friend back then, right?"

"Sure, okay." Daniel shifted in his seat as if he knew this story wasn't going to be short and sweet.

Mateo cringed inwardly at what would come next. He rubbed the back of his neck, then forced himself to continue. "Caroline reached out to me a few weeks ago. She insisted she was going to be in town visiting a friend and wanted to reconnect."

Daniel's only reaction was to lift a brow.

"I ignored her, of course. I didn't need that kind of toxicity in my life. But when I was in town one day getting flowers for Nikki..." He blew out a breath. "We bumped into each other, and she insisted she wanted to get me a coffee so she could apologize the right way."

A groan came from his friend, and he shook his head. "Big mistake."

Mateo shrugged. "Yeah, well, maybe I'm a glutton for punishment. She didn't even really apologize. I told her that I didn't want to see her, and I was happy with someone else. But she continued to try to see me. Even stopped by. I don't even know how she figured it out, but she realized I was seeing Nikki. She sent me a picture of Nikki having lunch with some guy."

The way Daniel was looking at him made him uneasy. It was like Daniel could already see where everything had gone wrong.

"What?" Mateo demanded.

"I can't believe you actually sat down with her."

"*That's* what you got from my story? Did you not hear that Nikki was having lunch with some dude? She said she was going to run some errands, and like an idiot, I agreed to babysit her kid while she went on a date."

Daniel didn't even flinch at his outburst. "Did she tell you why she was having lunch with that guy? What if it was a business meeting?"

Mateo's stomach dropped.

"Or what if he was an old friend or family member who wanted to catch up?" Daniel shrugged. "You seriously expect me to believe you trust Caroline?"

"Well, no, but—"

"And you showed Nikki the picture from Caroline?"

"Yeah, of course. I didn't want her to think I was being paranoid. I could tell she was pulling away—"

Daniel shifted and rested his forearm against the saddle

horn. "And what did Nikki say when she saw that you'd been messaging Caroline?"

"I haven't been messaging her!"

His friend rolled his eyes. "Okay, how did she react when she saw Caroline was messaging you?"

Mateo froze. She hadn't said anything. In fact, there hadn't been a lick of surprise on her face. It was almost as if she knew that Caroline had reached out to him. He groaned, pinching the bridge of his nose. Then he let out a curse. "I screwed up," he muttered.

"You sure did."

He shot Daniel a dark look.

"But just so we're on the same page, what exactly are you referring to?" Daniel smirked.

A sick and twisted feeling stirred in Mateo's midsection. He didn't want to believe it. In fact, the thought made him feel like he was going to retch right there. Nikki had tried to talk to him about Caroline as if she knew he needed some kind of closure, but he'd refused. He'd continued to kick that can down the road, so he didn't have to relive the feelings those memories stirred up. It was entirely possible Nikki read his refusal as an inability to move on—especially if she had figured out that he'd reconnected with Caroline.

"I never told her," Mateo rasped.

"Never told her what?"

"I never told Nikki that I'd bumped into Caroline. I figured it would be better if I kept it secret. I didn't think anything would come of it. Nikki kept insisting she wasn't Caroline's friend anymore." He tore his hat from his head and raked a hand through his hair. "She had to have figured it out." Mateo lifted his eyes to Daniel. "Nikki figured out that I saw Caroline. I don't know how, but she did." He let out a growl. "No wonder Nikki has been distant. She's probably thinking that I was interested in going back to Caroline."

Hot, fiery rage simmered within him at the possibility. It was all just assumptions at this point, but he wouldn't be surprised if he was right. This was the piece that had been missing.

A flicker of hope lit within him but was immediately doused as another revelation assaulted him. "It doesn't matter. I might have kept this from her, but she kept it from me to."

"What do you mean?" Daniel asked.

"I mean that she's been keeping secrets too."

Daniel sighed like someone might for an insolent child. "How do you know?"

"Because how else would Caroline have been at that restaurant? How else would she have known that I was dating Nikki? I never told her. I specifically kept that information from her because I didn't want her to retaliate. I know Caroline. I know the depths she would go to knock Nikki down a peg."

"And if you're right about Caroline's motives, you'd have to admit that this whole thing could be orchestrated."

Mateo shook his head. "Even if Caroline had a hand in setting this up, she wouldn't have been able to without connecting with Nikki. She doesn't live here. She came to visit a friend." And that friend could have been Nikki.

His heart was being torn in a million different directions. The betrayal. The fury. The desperation. Everything was culminating into one massive, angry bomb, and he wasn't sure what was going to happen when it finally exploded.

"Hey," Daniel murmured, drawing him out of his spiral.

"Let's say she was talking to Caroline. She's allowed to have friends, right? Even ones you despise."

But that was just it. Nikki had said so many times how much she disliked Caroline. They weren't friends. "Yeah, I guess," Mateo said.

"And if they weren't friends, she must have had a reason for meeting with Caroline. I mean, you got wrapped up in the chaos with that woman. No one knows better than you."

Mateo hated to admit that Daniel was sounding far too logical for his own good. There was only one problem. Mateo's heart had been destroyed too deeply for him to be able to march right back into a situation where he could get hurt again.

Before he could voice this, Sophia came running over. She was breathless and her face was red. Not only that, she looked madder than a hornet whose nest had been knocked down. "Mateo," she gasped. "I know what happened."

He shifted uncomfortably and glanced to Daniel.

"Caroline is sabotaging you and Nikki. She planned the whole thing, and it's all my fault."

"What do you mean it's your fault?" Mateo demanded. "What did you do?"

She winced, then shook her head. "That day she came to see you? I told her about Nikki. I wanted to rub it in her face. I think that's what pushed her over the edge." Her eyes darted to Daniel. "Rachel heard Caroline bragging about it at the salon. She said she was going to get you back and that she was going to make you forget all about Nikki." The fury in her eyes returned. "She said a lot of nasty stuff, Mateo. But it looks like she drew Nikki to the restaurant and asked the bartender to sit with Nikki, since she was upset or some nonsense."

Daniel cleared his throat, and Mateo didn't have to look at him to know that he was likely smugger than the first frog who learned to move on land. He was right. The guy in the picture wasn't Nikki's date.

Caroline had played them both.

And he'd messed everything up.

Would Nikki ever forgive him?

29

Nikki

Nikki poured over the classifieds, her headache pounding. It had been a week of searching and she hadn't managed to find anything that would come close to what she had right now. She threw down the newspaper with a sigh of disgust.

Who was she kidding? She wasn't going to be able to find anything that would work. No matter how desperate she was to no longer be under Mateo's roof, she wasn't willing to put Paxton in any sort of limbo. He'd been through too much for her to let that happen.

Even if she could find something close to what she had, there was little chance Mateo would give her a glowing reference. Maybe she needed to speak to Daniel. He was a supervisor of sorts. And he liked her well enough.

She groaned and pushed her hands into her hair. The last couple of weeks had been miserable. Knowing that

Mateo was lying about visiting with Caroline had taken its toll on her. Then keeping up with the lies of seeing her old friend had only added to it.

Well, Nikki had learned her lesson. Caroline had always been toxic, and she'd proven that she wasn't going to change.

Nikki went over the day that Mateo had broken things off with her a million times. That picture that Caroline had sent him—she'd been the mastermind behind it all. She'd said she was going to order more drinks, but she'd really only wanted to get Nikki into a position that would hurt Mateo.

And he'd believed Caroline.

Nikki didn't have any more tears left. Mateo had believed Caroline because they were already spending time together—reconciling. If he hadn't been interested in Caroline, he would have at least demanded that Nikki tell her story. Instead, he let her walk away.

And they hadn't spoken since.

A shuddering breath left Nikki's chest. She'd get through this. She'd been through breakups before. Paxton hadn't seemed to notice too much since he was still getting riding lessons from Mateo.

Maybe leaving wasn't the end goal. Maybe Nikki just needed to let the wound heal so she could move on. They could remain friends—as impossible as that appeared to be.

It would be impossible.

Yesterday, she'd locked eyes with Mateo, and for a brief moment she felt alive again, only to have him turn his back on her and for her to realize there would be no going back.

Her phone buzzed with a message, and Nikki glanced at the lit-up screen. Caroline's name populated it. That woman had been silent since that day at the restaurant. She hadn't reached out, and Nikki hadn't been interested either.

Whatever Caroline wanted to say, Nikki wasn't going to hear it.

She snatched up her phone and immediately blocked Caroline on all platforms. Next she deleted all her messages. If there was one destructive force on this planet that needed to be wiped out, it was Caroline.

Nikki tossed her phone onto the stainless steel countertop of the kitchen with disgust and sighed again. She didn't feel like cooking, but she'd have to start preparing dinner soon. Sure, she could have Jason and Mark whip something up, but that could put her job even more in jeopardy.

Mateo wouldn't fire her for breaking up with him, would he?

No. He was too good of a man for that.

But he would let her go if she started slipping.

What was she going to do?

Come on, Nikki. Wipe your crushed heart off the floor and keep going. You knew this was a possibility. You knew that Mateo was out of your league when you gave him your heart. Who else do you have to blame? No one.

Her eyes shifted to her phone again. There was only one reason Caroline would message her after everything.

She would be gloating. That's what she did. Once she got what she wanted, she made sure the world knew it.

Nikki's lips turned into a sneer as she considered what that might mean. If Caroline showed up at Winding Creek Ranch on Mateo's arm, that would be the end of everything. Nikki just didn't have the strength for it.

The door to the kitchen swung open and Sophia entered, looking frazzled. "Nikki, there you are. I've been looking for you."

Nikki lifted a brow and gestured to the kitchen. "Somehow, I think you knew this is exactly where I would be. It's sort of my job at the moment."

Not for long.

She couldn't think like that. She needed to be strong.

Not only for Paxton, but for herself.

Sophia moved closer to her and leaned her forearms atop the counter across from Nikki. The island in the middle of the kitchen was the perfect place to prep everything, and soon it would be covered with ingredients. But for now, it was the only barrier keeping the two of them separated. "I've been thinking a lot about last week."

Nikki stiffened. She'd asked Sophia to drop it. She didn't want to talk about Mateo or what had happened. Why was Sophia bringing it up now? Did she know something? Nikki's eyes slid to her phone, and now she found herself wishing she hadn't deleted the message from Caroline. Maybe there was a chance she could call the phone company to retrieve it.

"Nikki," Sophia said forcibly and reached for Nikki's hand. "You need to talk about it. You need to tell me what happened so I can help."

"You can't help though, Sophia. This isn't about you. This is about me and Mateo, and there's nothing that can be done." He wanted Caroline. He'd never denied it. And his actions had proved it.

Her friend squeezed her hand. "Look, I get it. He's got baggage, but Mateo—"

"I didn't care about his baggage, Sophia," she muttered with exasperation, tugging her hand free. "I cared about him. I..." Tears sprang to her eyes as the torrent of emotions burst out. "I loved him. He was everything to me. He made me feel..." She sucked in a shuddering breath. "He made me feel like I was the most beautiful girl in the world."

She turned away, hating the embarrassment that came with that confession. The insecurities she'd dealt with for her entire life had been laid out for Sophia's viewing pleasure, and now there was no hiding it.

"Nikki—" Sophia rounded the island, but Nikki stopped her.

"Don't. Okay? There's nothing to fix. If there was, it would have already happened. Honestly? I want to let it go. I'm tired of chasing something that isn't meant to be."

"You don't know that," she said quietly.

"But I do. You wouldn't understand." Nikki shut her eyes tight. Sophia was the epitome of perfection. She wasn't a stick by any means, but she was slender and toned. Her work with the horses had made her someone who turned heads wherever she went. Coupled with her dark hair and perfect skin tone—Sophia could have been a goddess in another life. She'd never grasp what Caroline had put Nikki through.

Thankfully, Sophia didn't argue. She simply pulled Nikki into her arms and held her tight. And for now, that was all Nikki needed.

SOPHIA: *Hey, I got a new horse today. He doesn't have a name. Think Paxton would want to do the honors?*

IT WAS GETTING LATE. Dinner had been cleaned up, and Paxton was coloring away in his book. Nikki glanced over at him and smiled. "Sophia has a surprise for you in the barn. You want to check it out?"

His head popped up, and his grin was the only thing worth living for. "Really? Is she getting me a horse?"

Nikki laughed, holding out her hand. "No. Sorry, bud, but we don't have the money for something like that. But it's close."

He frowned with concentration. "What is it?"

"It's a surprise, silly," she poked him in the ribs, and he laughed as he held his stomach.

They walked hand in hand toward the barn, and Nikki glanced around them. She knew she shouldn't be looking for Mateo, but she'd seen him only once today, and that was on her way to start lunch. She'd forced herself to look away before he caught her staring. Nikki was so over the embarrassment of longing for someone who would never want her in the same way.

She thought it would have been easier by now. But apparently her heart wasn't ready to let go.

Paxton glanced up at her, and she squeezed his hand as she smiled back. He was her whole world now. She'd focus on that and nothing else.

Sophia waved them over, grinning broadly. "He's over here."

Paxton released Nikki's hand and ran forward. "Who?"

"The new horse." Sophia glanced at Nikki, and something in her eyes said there was more to what was happening. "I've already got him saddled for you. But you need to pick a name."

Paxton stared at her with wide eyes. "I get to name him?"

She nodded. "You get to name him, kiddo."

Paxton scrunched up his face with concentration after

getting a good look at the chestnut horse. "Mmm. How about..." he drawled. "Dragon."

Sophia laughed. "That's quite a name."

"It is," Nikki agreed.

"I think it's perfect," a low, timbered voice uttered behind her.

Nikki jumped, and Paxton turned to smile at the one person she wasn't ready to see up close. Mateo's fingertips brushed against hers, and she sucked in sharply.

"What do you say I help you take him for a ride in the corral?" Sophia asked, her eyes landing on Nikki. She was going to be sorry for this.

"Can I, Mom?" Paxton asked. "Mateo says I'm good enough to start working with my own horse now. Right, Mateo?"

Nikki stiffened, not wanting to turn around to look the man she still loved in the eye.

This time his voice was close.

Too close.

It came right behind her left ear, and it set off a wave of goosebumps all across her arms. "Absolutely."

Before she knew what was happening, Sophia was leading Paxton past her and Mateo toward the door.

Nikki spun to follow, but Mateo stepped into her path, his broad body cutting her off. She lifted her chin to meet those eyes, and the world all but fell away at her feet. "Sorry," she mumbled, attempting to move past him. But he sidestepped again. She frowned. "What do you need, Mateo?"

He cleared his throat, and the Adam's apple at his throat bobbed. "We need to talk."

She shook her head. "No, we don't. We both said everything we needed to."

"I need to ask you one more question."

Nikki dropped her gaze to a spot just over his shoulder. "Fine. What is it?"

"Do you love me?"

Against her will, her eyes darted to meet his. She'd never been a good liar, and she knew if she denied it, he'd know. It wasn't even worth trying. "I don't see what that has anything to do with—"

He stepped into her, his voice huskier than before. "Do. You. Love. Me?"

Her throat dried up and closed all at once. She couldn't breathe. This wasn't fair. He'd plunged a knife into her chest, and now he was twisting it. "You know I do," she rasped. "I think I always have." Fury laced the last couple of words.

Mateo tilted his head, studying her.

Hot, angry tears burned her eyes, and she shook her head when he didn't say anything more. "I have to go—"

His arm reached out and he gently wrapped his fingers around her wrist, stopping her escape. "I've kept so many secrets from you," he whispered. "So many secrets that I should have just shared. Then we wouldn't be in this mess."

She scoffed. "Yeah, like the fact that you were seeing Caroline."

He flinched, and she almost felt guilty for hitting that nerve. "You were in communication with her too, were you not?"

Her brows lifted, and her face burned with guilt and indignation. "I was..." She gritted her teeth and looked away, attempting to pull her arm from his grasp. "Let me go, Mateo," she begged. "*Please.*"

With his free hand, he reached out and traced a finger

along her jaw. She didn't even have the strength to pull her away.

"You're right," he said, and her heart sagged with pain. "I should have told you that Caroline was trying to reconnect. But it was very much one-sided."

She jerked her chin away from his touch with a huff. "That's not what she said."

He closed his eyes as if praying for the strength to finish this conversation. "You and I both know how senseless it is to believe anything that comes from her mouth."

Nikki stopped her attempt to retreat. He was right. Caroline knew how to twist things. She lifted her eyes to meet his. "But I saw you. I saw the flowers you gave her. She was the girl from your past—"

His hold on her wrist tightened. "*You.* You were the girl from my past, Nikki. Don't you get it? You were the girl that I couldn't get out of my head. You were the person who was worth another broken heart. You were the only one capable of making me want to try again—to have a family."

Her mouth parted. "What?"

Mateo tugged her closer, his other hand now clasped against the side of her neck as he brushed a forgotten tear with his thumb. "You were the crush who got away," he whispered. "You are the beautiful, kind, spirited woman who makes me feel like anything is possible. You don't know how sorry I am for not telling you the truth about that day—the day I bumped into Caroline. Those flowers were for you, and she'd made me so mad that I forgot to grab them on my way out."

Nikki shivered. The note had been for her? He'd wanted something with her for all of these years? She would have laughed at the impossibility of it, but then there would be no explanation for why he was here pouring his heart out to her.

"I should have never let Caroline get into my head. I should have trusted you." Pain laced his voice. "You've never done anything to warrant me not giving you the benefit of the doubt."

Except she had. She'd lied about meeting Caroline. They both had. The irony of that situation wasn't lost on her, and she let out a disparaging laugh. So much pain and suffering could have been avoided if she'd come clean about seeing her. "I thought..." She shut her eyes, and more tears spilled. "I thought you were still in love with her."

Mateo made a disgruntled sound, and she peered up at him to see him making a disgusted face to match it. "I would *never* choose her again." He released her and cupped her face with both hands. "I would *never* choose anyone over you."

Her chest burned. The smoldering embers of the relationship they'd been building had new life breathed into it.

"I love you, Nikki. I never stopped loving you. I came here to ask you for another chance." He sucked in a deep breath and released it heavily. "But I'd understand if you don't want to give it to me."

"Mateo," she whispered, reaching up to touch his face.

"Please," he said, leaning into her touch. "Let me spend the rest of my life proving just how much I love—"

She cut him off with her lips, capturing his mouth in a searing kiss that neither one of them would soon forget. It was pain, heartache, hope, and forgiveness all wrapped up in one.

Mateo scooped her into his arms, holding her like he was afraid she'd disappear at any second. There was a desperation in the way he kissed her back, to the way he clung to her.

And it mirrored her own.

He pulled away just enough to press his forehead to hers. "Tell me you're mine."

Nikki hesitated for only a moment. "I'm yours," she murmured breathlessly.

"Only mine, and not some bartender's in town," he added.

A smile tugged at her lips, and she feathered her fingers through his hair. "Only yours," she whispered just before stealing another kiss.

EPILOGUE

One year later

Mateo

"This is great. I'm sure all the guys are thrilled."

"You sure?" Mateo let his focus sweep across the crowd of people in their backyard. They'd invited all their employees, a couple of new hires, their families, and clients.

Sophia nodded, bumping her shoulder into his. "Positive. What better way to show your appreciation for everyone who's making this ranch great. We're really going somewhere." That last part was said with so much awe that Mateo couldn't help but look down at his sister.

She grinned at him with emotion shining in her eyes. "And that's all thanks to you."

He pulled her close, wrapping his arm around her neck and using his free hand to give her a noogie.

Sophia screeched and attempted to scramble out of his grasp, but his hold was too tight. "I'm not a kid anymore, Mateo! Gah!" She finally succeeded in escaping his grasp, her eyes shooting venom.

Mateo laughed, turning his attention to the people surrounding them. He'd always felt like an outsider, but for the first time in a long while, he felt like he had a place where he belonged.

His attention zoned in on the one person who seemed to be key to that. She could always sense his gaze, and at that moment, her eyes met his.

Warmth flooded his entire being when she stared at him like that.

Sophia dug her elbow into his side, and he yelped. "What was that for?" He rubbed the offensive spot.

She smirked at him, then turned her focus to Nikki. They were several yards away from her, standing near the house while she hovered at the food table. "When are you going to take the leap?"

"What do you mean?"

"It's been a year, Mateo. She's not Caroline."

His smile felt plastered to his face as he attempted to calm his racing heart. "I know that."

"She's not going to leave you for someone else. And Caroline gave up tormenting y'all months ago."

"What are you trying to say?" he asked weakly.

"I'm trying to find out if you're going to make an honest woman out of her and ask her to be your wife."

He hated how much that question gave him anxiety.

They were in a good place—had been for months. It was comfortable and easy. But Sophia was right. Mateo had come to that same conclusion two months ago when he'd bought the ring. He just hadn't gotten the courage to actually do it.

"She's perfect for you, Mateo," she said softly.

Mateo raked a hand through his hair and sighed. "Yeah, I know."

"And you love that kid."

That brought a smile to his face. "He's a neat kid."

"So, what's the hold-up?"

He made a face.

"Uh-oh." Sophia teased.

"*What*?"

"You're *scared*."

"I'm *not* scared," he argued.

Sophia snickered. "Yes, you are. You're scared to get married. What is it? You can't be scared that she's going to leave you. Is it the wedding day?"

He stilled. That was it. She made an excellent point. The thought of planning a big wedding and having to stand in front of a group of friends and family terrified him. It made him sick just thinking about it. Mateo turned to his sister and grabbed her by her upper arms. "You're a genius!" He kissed her on the forehead and hurried away, ignoring her snarky comeback.

Mateo immediately sought out Paxton. He'd been waiting for the right time to talk to the kid about his plans. If Paxton knew too soon, he was bound to let the secret slip. Now, Mateo was ready. And if Paxton wasn't, they could wait until he was.

Paxton was standing on a rung of a corral fence near the barn, watching his new horse. Dragon had a spunky personality, but he adored Paxton. Mateo could see it in the way they worked together.

Mateo slowed his steps as he approached, then leaned against the rail at the boy's side. "Hey, bud."

Paxton glanced up at him and smiled.

"I wanted to ask you something if that's okay. Actually, a couple somethings." Part of this conversation had a lot more to do with Paxton than Nikki. The boy needed to know just how much he meant to him.

"Okay," Paxton said eagerly. "Are we going to talk about riding?"

Slowly, Mateo shook his head. "Actually, it has to do with you."

Paxton frowned. "Me? Am I in trouble?"

He chuckled. "No, of course not. It has to do with your mom and me, too."

His frown remained, and a crease formed between his brows. "Okay," he hedged.

Mateo dropped down so he was eye-level with the boy. "Did you know that I love you?"

A hesitant smile spread across Paxton's lips. "Yeah. And you love Mom, too."

"I sure do," Mateo agreed. "And do you know what men do when there are people they love?"

Paxton tilted his head. "You take care of them."

Mateo ruffled the kid's hair. "You're too smart for your own good."

The smile that boy wore could have set off rocket ships; it was so full of bright energy.

"Anyway, since I love you and your mom, I want to make you part of my family."

Paxton's smile changed to surprise, and it took all of Mateo's courage to continue.

"I want to marry your mom." His throat closed up as he forced himself to add, "And I want to adopt you—make you mine. Because you've become like a son to me—"

Paxton dropped from the corral and flung his arms around Mateo's neck. He buried his face into Mateo's neck, and his shoulders shook. Was he crying? Laughing?

"Hey, hey, hey," Mateo murmured, drawing backward.

A tear speckled Paxton's cheek.

"What's the matter?"

"You..." Paxton bit his lower lip. "You want to be my dad?"

Mateo sighed with relief, a smile tugging at his lips. "Yeah, bud. I want to be your dad. Is that okay?"

He nodded. "Yeah."

"Do you want to come with me to ask your mom?"

Paxton's eyes widened, and again, he nodded. "Yeah," he whispered. "She's gonna be so excited."

"I hope so, kiddo." Mateo stood and held out his hand to Paxton. "Come on. Let's go find her."

"Come on, Mom. You have to come over here." Paxton was playing his role perfectly. Their plan was to lure Nikki away so no one would know what was happening—namely Sophia.

Mateo could hear Nikki laugh even though she was out

of sight. Their shuffled footsteps drew closer and closer until Paxton dragged his mother around the side of the barn.

Paxton grinned, and Nikki stared at Mateo with surprise.

He'd already gotten down on one knee, and he held up the ring for her to see. She brought her hands to her mouth with a gasp, her wide eyes darting from Mateo to the ring, to Paxton and back. "What…"

"You are the love of my life," Mateo started, "the dream of my past and the light of my future. There is no one I want to spend my life with more than you." His eyes dipped to Paxton momentarily. "Both of you."

Nikki pulled Paxton closer to her, and emotion brimmed in her eyes as he stared at him.

Mateo's voice shook. "I already feel like you're part of my family, but I think we need to make it official." He gestured with the ring. "What do you say? We could get out of here."

"What? Now?" Nikki gasped. "We need—"

He got to his feet and pulled her into him, brushing his lips to her temple. "All I need is you. We could go now—fly to Vegas and be married before tomorrow. We could slip off to the mountains and find a priest to help us. I don't need a big wedding." He pulled back enough to look her in the eye. "I. Just. Need. You."

Her smile melted him from the inside out. "I couldn't have said it better myself." She tilted her head. "But I do think your siblings would skin you alive if they weren't invited, especially Sophia… so maybe we make a plan that includes them."

He groaned, which brought a laugh to her lips. "Fine. But we're getting married before the month is over." He smiled down at Paxton. "I can't wait to be a dad."

"Who's that?" Nikki said as they walked back toward the backyard party.

"Hmm?" Mateo wouldn't release Nikki. His arm remained around her waist, and his other hand gripped one of Paxton's. He was on a completely different kind of high right now, and anything anyone said to him might actually go over his head. Nikki was going to be his.

"The guy Sophia is talking to."

His eyes shifted to where Nikki pointed.

Sophia looked livid. Her whole body was stiff, and her face looked like it had been carved out of stone. The man's demeanor, on the other hand, was more relaxed. He smirked at her while she railed into him about something.

Mateo watched for a moment, then when Nikki nudged him, he murmured, "Cameron Walker."

"Does Sophia know him? Why is he here?"

"He's a new hire. I don't think they know each other. I met him last summer when I went to an auction. He's been making waves in the breeding world. It's actually amazing, the work he does."

Nikki rested her cheek against Mateo's shoulder. "It sort of looks like they know each other."

He continued to watch their interaction with interest. Then he shook his head. "Nah. Cam would have told me if he knew her. He's been here a couple days. And it doesn't take much for someone to get under Sophia's skin. He probably said something she found offensive."

"Hmm..." Nikki said, not continuing the conversation further.

He turned his attention to his fiancée, a huge smile on

his face that would likely be there the rest of his life with Nikki as his bride. "Come on. Let's go save him from whatever nonsense Sophia has him involved in and tell her the good news!"

~

HELLO SWEET ROMANCE READER!

I hope you loved watching Mateo and Nicole fall in love —and how little Paxton managed to steal everyone's hearts.

Ready for another unforgettable Palmer love story? This time it's Sophia's turn...

She had a week-long fling with a handsome horse breeder five years ago—and a broken heart to show for it. Now Cameron Walker is back, working on her family's ranch, and Sophia can't decide if she wants to kiss him or chase him off with a pitchfork.

Don't miss the fiery sparks and second chances in *Sophia & Cameron*, the next Palmers of Copper Creek book!

Buy the paperback version of **Sophia & Cameron, Palmers of Copper Creek Book Two,** on Amazon! Soon, paperbacks will also be available on my store, Natalie Dean Books (nataliedeanbooks.com). Be sure to check there first!

ABOUT THE AUTHOR

Born and raised in a small coastal town in the south, I was raised to treasure family and love the Lord. I'm a dedicated homeschooling mom who loves to travel and spend time with my growing-up-too-fast son.

When I'm not busy writing or running my business, you can find me cleaning house, cooking dinner, feeding our three rescue cats, trying to make learning fun and coaxing my son to pick up his toys. On less busy days, you may also find me paddling down a spring run in Florida, hiking a mountain trail in Georgia (on the rare vacation to the mountains), or enjoying a book.

If you love Natalie Dean books, you can be notified of new releases by signing up to my newsletter at nataliedea nauthor.com, where you will also receive two free short stories for signing up. Just click on the "Free Books" tab at the top and you'll be on your way!

Also, as previously mentioned, I've opened my own online bookstore and I'd love your support! As of May 2025, I'm selling ebooks, audiobooks and paperbacks at Natalie Dean Books. By late summer or fall 2025, I should large print paperbacks available as well. At the request of my loyal readers, I'll also be adding merchandise, such as glasses, cups, magnets and more. So come check out my small mom-owned author business at nataliedeanbooks.com.

You can also scan the QR code below to be taken to the home page of Natalie Dean Books.

facebook.com/nataliedeanromance

9 781964 875590